SHADOW

PROTECTORS
UNDERCOVER
—TEAM ONE—

BOOK FIVE

USA TODAY BESTSELLING AUTHOR

HEATHER SLADE

UNDERCOVER SHADOW
Copyright © 2025

This book is a work of fiction. All names, characters, locations, and incidents are products of the authors' imaginations. Any resemblance to actual persons, things, living or dead, locales, or events is entirely coincidental.

979-8-88649-625-3

Table of Contents

Chapter 1 1

Chapter 2 7

Chapter 3 24

Chapter 4 52

Chapter 5 66

Chapter 6 84

Chapter 7 100

Chapter 8 118

Chapter 9 137

Chapter 10 161

Chapter 11 182

Chapter 12 200

Chapter 13 224

Chapter 14 242

Chapter 15 254

Chapter 16 271

Chapter 17 290

Chapter 18 304

Chapter 19 332

Epilogue 342

Commanded 355

About the Author 363

1

Nightingale

I stared out at the London sky, finding no stars tonight, only darkness broken by the city's endless lights. From my safe-house window in Notting Hill, I tracked the shadows moving across the wet pavement below, mentally cataloging each suspicious figure. My breath created small patches of fog on the cold glass, temporary markers of my existence that disappeared seconds later.

They were following me again tonight. Different faces, same purpose. They weren't even trying to be subtle anymore.

My mobile vibrated—the third burner this week. The text contained only coordinates and a time—zero one thirty. Half an hour from now. Another move, another location, another step in this elaborate game where I couldn't identify all the players. The message came from Kestrel, an encrypted handle I'd come to dread. Another ghost pulling my strings.

My gaze drifted to the small tracking device I'd extracted from my tactical vest after Syria. I'd disabled it, of course, but hadn't destroyed it.

If I'd left it active, Tag would have found me by now. Niall MacTaggert—the man I'd trusted more than anyone was also the man who'd put it on me, in the first place.

The thought of him sent a familiar ache through my chest. He'd be pacing his study at Glenshadow by now, his green eyes intense as he tracked intelligence feeds, searching for any trace of me. Tag didn't abandon his people. Especially not someone he'd promised to protect.

I turned away from the window, methodically packing the few possessions I could bring with me. Everything fit into a single backpack—the mark of an operative who knew better than to grow attached to physical things.

Or people.

My fingers paused on a faded photograph, its edges worn from frequent handling. Two figures stood before a Highland backdrop—Tag and Idris, arms slung over each other's shoulders, laughing at something outside the frame.

I slipped the photo into my jacket pocket alongside the letter I'd carried for three years—Idris' last gift, his final mission. It had led me here, to London, to Damascus before that, always one step behind the people who'd killed my brother. Idris had told me to go to Tag, to trust him with everything he'd sent me. But I'd been nineteen and shattered and determined to finish what my brother began. Alone.

"You shouldn't keep that," a woman's voice said from the doorway.

I didn't startle. I'd known she was there before she spoke—the subtle shift in the air pressure, the nearly imperceptible creak of the floorboard.

Viper stepped into the room, and I closed my hand around the picture. "What are you doing here?" I asked.

"Your tails have gotten more aggressive. They've stepped up their movement in the last hour—as if they're preparing to close in."

"How many?"

"Two that we've tracked. Could be more. One we believe is Obsidian. We still don't have ID on the other—could be Janus', could be the Russian, could be McLaren's asset if she's actually alive."

He'd found me after all. "So I go dark again."

"Yes. An MI6 extraction team is on the way. They'll be there in sixty minutes and will take you to another secure location until we can figure out who these people are and what they want."

Little did she know that I'd be long gone by then.

"You know Obsidian won't stop," I said. "He'll keep searching."

"The Earl of Glenshadow is persistent, I grant you," Viper responded, moving toward the doorway she'd come in through. "But he's following the breadcrumbs we've intentionally placed. By the time he realizes the trail is false, it will be too late."

I turned toward the window, hiding my expression. "You underestimate him."

"Perhaps." She sounded amused. "Or perhaps you overestimate his feelings for you. Men like MacTaggert love the chase more than the capture."

I didn't respond to the barb. Let her believe what she wanted about my relationship with Tag. The less she understood, the better.

She checked her mobile. "Our contact will be arriving sooner than anticipated. Be ready." She paused at the doorway. "And, Agent Nassar? Do remember where your loyalties lie now."

When her footsteps faded, I extracted a small tool from my boot heel and pried up a floorboard beneath the bed. Inside the shallow space lay a second communications device—neither standard MI6 nor Unit 23 issue, but something more specialized.

I activated it and composed a message in the unique encryption protocol only a handful of people in the world could decrypt. My warning needed to be clear without revealing too much.

Janus active. McLaren remains in play. Tunnels vital.

I hesitated, thumb hovering over the send button, hating what I'd sacrificed to infiltrate what remained of the Labyrinth network. Even the simplest of warnings were cloak and dagger.

I sent the message, then disassembled the device, scattering its components in different locations around the room—the heating vent, the toilet tank, the hollow curtain rod. Nothing recognizable would remain when they searched the place after my departure.

Outside, a car engine turned over. Across the road, a figure stepped from the shadows, eyes tilted upward toward my window.

I recognized the silhouette, and my heart froze.

Tag.

He'd found me, despite Viper's breadcrumbs intended to lead him astray.

But he couldn't approach now—not with them watching. Not with what I had to accomplish.

I stepped back from the window, out of sight, my decision made before I fully processed my options. Retrieving the burner phone, I typed the message to be relayed to the teams sent to extract me.

ABORT. COMPROMISED. MOVING EAST.

I destroyed the mobile, scattered the pieces in various places like I had the other, then gathered my backpack, checked my weapon, and slipped into the hallway.

By the time Tag breached the flat, I would be gone.

Again.

2

Tag

My weapon was already drawn when I kicked in the safe-house door, splintering it with my boot before sweeping inside. Weeks of tracking, of following ghosts through London's shadows, and I'd finally found her. Or thought I had. I cleared the rooms one by one, finding each empty. The bed didn't appear slept in, but an indent on the sofa suggested she'd been waiting. For her handler? For extraction? For me?

"Fuck," I muttered under my breath. How in the hell had she gotten out of here without my spotting her?

Frustration burned in my chest as I lowered my gun, picked up a teacup that sat on the kitchen counter, and held its warmth against my palm. Even her scent—musk, spice, wood, and oud—lingered in the air.

I glanced at an open window, where the February wind shifted the curtains. It was big enough for her to crawl out of. Was it a clue like the burner phone that lay crushed in the sink beneath it, SIM card gone?

It had been three weeks since Nightingale went underground after discovering evidence that Project Labyrinth was still operational. Days of her in danger while I tore London apart, searching.

And she'd slipped through my fingers again.

"Damn it, Leila," I muttered as I exited the way I assumed she had. The window was almost too small for me to fit through, but I'd managed tougher escape routes.

I pulled out my phone, already moving down the stairs, headed out to resume my search.

The Unit 23 surveillance network gave me access to every CCTV camera in central London, so I worked from my vehicle, laptop balanced on the seat beside me as I followed her digital footprints through the city.

I knew her patterns because I'd been the one to train her. When cornered, Leila would head to the closest transportation hub. King's Cross would give her rail connections north; Eurostar if she needed to leave the country entirely.

Sure enough, an Oyster card registered to one of the aliases she'd given me what felt like an eternity ago pinged at zero two hundred, so I knew she'd taken the Tube's Northern Line toward King's Cross from Notting Hill.

As I navigated through empty streets, following her digital trail through the surveillance feeds, memories of the first time I met Leila replayed in my mind.

***

Rain drummed against the black umbrellas held by those of us present to witness Idris Nassar's burial. The gathering was small—intelligence operatives didn't get military honors or public ceremonies. There were only a handful of us who actually knew what he did for a living.

Con stood beside me, rain running off his umbrella in steady streams. We'd both worked dozens of operations with Idris over the past two years, mainly joint missions between Syrian and British intelligence. He'd become more than a liaison between agencies. He was our friend.

The young woman standing at the graveside had his hazel eyes that sometimes turned dark as night, like now, giving nothing away even in grief. Leila Nassar wore her brother's loss like armor. Her spine remained straight despite the weight crushing down on her. Her hair was plastered to her cheeks from the downpour, but she didn't move to push it away. Nineteen years old, and she'd already lost everyone. Her father and mother—a Syrian intelligence officer and a British MI6 analyst—had died in a Damascus terrorist bombing a year ago. They'd been at the wrong place at the wrong time. Now, she'd lost Idris too.

The last time I'd spoken to him, three weeks before he died in the same city, he'd seemed distracted. He asked questions about weapons technology and neural interfaces, both things outside his usual scope. When I pressed, he deflected, saying he was following a lead, but had nothing concrete yet.

"Promise me something," he'd said as we parted. "If anything happens to me, look after Leila."

The request had caught me off guard—Idris wasn't the type to ask for promises.

"You have my word."

"I mean it, Tag. I'm all she has. If something goes wrong…"

"Nothing's going to go wrong."

But it had. And now, I understood—he'd known he was in danger. He'd been trying to tell me without saying it outright. And I'd failed to see it.

I'd read Leila's file often enough to know it by heart. She and Idris had private tutors from a very young age, who prepared them for foreign service. The two spoke several languages fluently, including Arabic, English, Russian, Farsi, and French. As they got older, they received military and intelligence training in combat and cryptanalysis as well.

"Her mother and I worked together when we were both starting out." Typhon's voice was rough when he approached me at the end of the service. "She asked me to look after both her children if anything happened to her or her husband. I failed at that, didn't I?"

The weight of his words mirrored my own about Leila. I'd made a vow I'd do everything I could to keep, but what if I failed in the same way we'd all failed her brother?

After the few others left, Typhon and I approached her together.

"Ms. Nassar," I said in a quiet tone. "I'm Niall MacTaggert, and this is Commander Marras. Your brother worked with us."

She studied us, not attempting to hide that she read us the way her parents and brother had taught her, cataloging everything she saw—the way we stood and the weight of the weapons under our coats.

"I know who you are." Her accent held traces of both London and Damascus. "Obsidian, Typhon, Infidel, and Savior."

Code names. So Idris had trusted her with that much.

"He spoke of you often," Typhon said. "Proudly."

Her eyes locked on mine as she nodded.

"You're one of us now," Typhon added. "If you want to be."

"What does that mean?" she asked.

"Your brother requested that you be given a position within MI6. Actually, Unit 23, but you'll have to work your way up."

She shook her head and raised her chin. "Unit 23 or nothing."

Typhon's eyes scrunched, and he studied her for several seconds. "Very well. First, you'll attend training at our facility in Scotland," he agreed. "Obsidian will oversee your progress. If you pass the evaluation, you're in."

"When I pass," she corrected. Not with arrogance, with certainty.

Neither Typhon nor I challenged her statement.

Less than a month later, she walked into the private training center. Six months after that, she proved herself in her first field op in Damascus.

***

Now, three years later, I still called her "kid" because it was the only way I could maintain distance from a woman who saw too much and made me feel too much.

I abandoned my car and ran after spotting her at King's Cross station, where multiple cameras showed her moving amongst other late-night travelers. She wore a black jacket with the hood up, but I knew her walk. She was headed toward Platform 9, where the Highland Sleeper to Scotland was scheduled to depart in twelve minutes.

My hand closed around her upper arm when I caught her at the barriers just as she lifted her ticket to scan it. She didn't flinch, didn't struggle. Her muscles coiled under my grip, ready to strike if needed, but she held still.

"Running north?" I asked.

"I expected you hours ago."

I smirked but didn't respond, knowing she probably had.

"We need to move. Now," I said, reading the brief message that had appeared from Typhon. *Do not board. Transport arranged. Make contact ASAP.* Unlike Leila, I'd allowed him to track me.

I nodded once, knowing he'd pick it up through whichever camera he was currently monitoring.

She studied me while I speed-dialed.

"Obsidian," Typhon said, answering on the second ring. "I've arranged for immediate extraction. Renegade's family has a place in the Highlands on the North Sea. Dunravin Castle is both isolated and defensible. Transport is on the way."

"Copy that."

"Tag." He paused. "Keep her safe."

"Always."

"Where are we going?" she asked when I ended the call and led her out of the station.

"Dunravin."

My mobile buzzed with a message from Renegade. *City Airport. Hangar 7. Weather system moving in fast. Window closing.*

"Transport's waiting," I said.

She nodded as if in surrender, but I knew better. Leila would never. She'd withdraw. Strategically.

As promised, the helicopter waited at London City Airport's private terminal with its rotors already warming. The pilot gave a brief signal as we climbed aboard. Leila sat across from me in the dim cabin, analyzing everything, including the flight path on the pilot's screen and the atmospheric chaos apparent on radar.

"We'll be trapped there if that front hits." She raised her voice to speak over the rotor noise.

"So be it."

"We should abort. Find another location."

"Not an option," I countered

The advancing storm was unusually massive for February. We'd have maybe eighteen hours before it hit the area where we were headed, if that's where it made landfall. If it did, there'd be no extraction for days. There'd also be no way for whoever was following her to get to us. That was the most important part of the equation.

Neither of us left the chopper when we landed in Edinburgh two and a half hours later and the ground crew refueled it.

"Remember Buda?" she said so quietly I could barely hear her. "Where I had to wear that ridiculous dress."

"Of course I do." We'd been undercover in Hungary, attending an event at the castle where a member of the former royal family was targeted for assassination. It felt like a lifetime ago, but no matter how long I lived, I'd never forget how Leila looked in the dress she'd called ridiculous but I thought was the sexiest thing I'd ever seen.

"Change of plans," the pilot announced through the comms, interrupting a recollection that should've been forbidden. He motioned to a jet that approached from our right.

We quickly exited one aircraft and boarded the other.

"Wind gusts are building fast. I'll be able to land at Dornoch Airfield," said the pilot, who I recognized as being former RAF. "But once there, I'll have a tight window to get in and out."

"Copy that," I responded, knowing that, when we touched down, Typhon would have a vehicle waiting on the tarmac.

I followed Leila into the main cabin and waited until she chose a seat, then took the one across the aisle and studied the woman who had been under my skin since her first day of intensive training at Unit 23's facility near Cape Wrath in the Durness parish—less than two hours north of the castle where we were headed.

Then and now, I had to remain steadfast in not succumbing to the overwhelming attraction I had for her. She was Idris' sister, I reminded myself again and again. That meant hands-off, regardless of how impossible it was to keep my thoughts from drifting to her.

I couldn't ignore the way her body naturally turned toward mine in the jet's cabin that felt too small, too intimate. Every movement as she adjusted herself in her seat made the black athletic shirt she wore shift across her body, drawing my attention despite my attempts to look anywhere else. The fabric pulled tighter when she reached for her seat belt, outlining the curves of her ample breasts and the dip of her waist. The way her long hair was pulled into a tight bun exposed the elegant line of her neck, and the cargo pants that had seemed practical in the underground station now felt designed to torture me.

She glanced over and caught me staring at the spot where her pulse flickered beneath her bronze skin. Every time I was near her, I fought to remain detached, but with her close enough to touch, my resolve threatened to unravel. To fall away in the same way her clothes would as I peeled them from her body.

"Tag?" she said as my eyes swept her breasts once more, unable to resist one last glimpse but nearly biting my tongue when her hardened nipples kept my gaze lingering overly long.

I cleared my throat. "Yes?"

"Never mind."

From the corner of my eye, I caught the flush of her cheeks before she turned her head toward the window. I rested my head against the seat and silently repeated the words that had become my mantra.

She was Idris' sister. She was twenty-two to my thirty-four. She was my responsibility to protect. It could never be more than that. We *could not* be together. It didn't matter how magnetic the pull between us was.

I knew better than to succumb. I'd learned not to from my parents, who'd taught me what happened when people who shouldn't be together tried to force it. The vow I'd made at my dad's funeral held—never marry, never risk becoming them.

I didn't open my eyes until the plane touched down at the private airstrip at Dornoch. As anticipated, a Land Rover waited with keys in the ignition and basic supplies loaded in the back.

The drive north to Dunravin took less than ten minutes through the Highland predawn twilight. The road narrowed as we climbed to where the castle sat, high on the cliff where there was nothing but the historic edifice, tempestuous sky, and the smell of the sea.

"The storm is moving in faster than predicted," Leila observed as clouds raced across the moon.

The radio confirmed it with severe weather warnings, recommendations to seek shelter, and advisories to avoid unnecessary travel. The forecaster predicted that by tomorrow night, the Highlands would be entirely cut off from the outside world.

"What do you know about this place?" Nightingale asked as I drove through the gates that had been left open.

"Renegade said the place was solid but needed work. The heat functions well enough in the east wing, but is intermittent everywhere else."

The driveway curved, and Dunravin Castle came into view, its towers and battlements showing little of what it had withstood during six centuries of Highland squalls. Even as old as it was, it was formidable.

"Christ," Leila breathed.

"Gothic enough for you?"

"I was thinking more 'defensible position with too many unknowns,' but sure. Let's go with Gothic."

I parked as close as I could to the entrance, and we raced to the main door. It was constructed of massive oak reinforced with iron and opened with a key old enough that it should belong in a museum. Inside, the main hall was shrouded in shadows until I found the lights.

"There's supposed to be a generator in the undercroft," I said. "Solar panels with battery backup."

"Solar," she muttered, rolling her eyes. "Zero redundancy."

Leila moved farther inside, cataloging exits and evaluating positions. With every step, she appeared more exhausted, running on fumes, yet thinking strategically.

"Renegade said there are four bedrooms in the east section," I said, reading more of the message I'd received from him.

She paused at a window and gazed out at the sea. The wind was picking up, rattling the centuries-old glass. "How long has it been since his family was here?"

"No idea. My guess is it's too isolated for regular use," I responded.

"And yet ideally isolated for hiding someone being hunted."

"Exactly."

She turned from the window, and for an instant, her composure slipped. I saw what the last few weeks had cost her—the fear she'd never admit to caused by the weight of whatever she'd discovered in Syria.

"We should talk about—"

"Whatever it is can wait until we've both had a chance to rest."

"There's vital intel," she pressed.

"Most of which I probably already know."

She raised a brow.

"Let me rephrase. I probably know some."

As I followed her up the grand staircase, I tried to look anywhere other than at the way her arse swayed with every step she took. The woman was solid muscle, yet no amount of fitness could ever hide her femininity. As I did every time I was with her, I longed to pull her into my arms, not in a brotherly hug, but as a man who desired her more than I had any other woman.

"It's freezing up here," Leila said as we reached the top of the staircase. She opened the first door we came to, which led to a large bedroom that had a massive rock fireplace already laid with wood.

"Wait here," I said, moving past her to check the room. It was the master suite, by the look of it, with heavy furniture built to last centuries, thick draperies on the windows, tapestries hung on the walls, and a sofa positioned near doors that led to a balcony. The bed, which sat farther from the hearth, was massive, with carved posts reaching nearly to the ceiling.

The lights flickered, died, then came on at half strength as I knelt to put a match to the kindling.

"I'll sort the generator in the morning. Tonight, we'll stay here, where there's heat." I stood, brushing my hands clean. "I'll take the sofa. Get some rest."

She was already moving toward the bed, exhaustion winning over any argument. She climbed in fully clothed and pulled the heavy blankets up to her chin.

The archaic heating system groaned somewhere in the walls, then went noiseless.

Twenty minutes later, the room remained so cold I could see my breath, and the sofa might as well have been carved from ice.

"Tag?" Her voice sounded small from across the room.

"Yeah?"

"You're going to freeze over there."

"I'm fine."

"No, you're not. I can hear your teeth chattering." A pause. "Please get in the bed. We'll freeze separately or survive together."

She was right. Hypothermia wouldn't help anyone. I stood and moved to the opposite side from where she lay, then crawled between the layers of blankets rather than under them.

"Thank you," she whispered.

The wind howled. The wood crackled. And I lay there, acutely aware of every breath she took, trying not to think about how many days we'd be trapped here and how absolutely fucked I likely was.

3

Nightingale

My consciousness returned in layers—warmth first, then weight, then the shocking realization that I was wrapped in Tag's arms.

Though we were still in yesterday's wrinkled, musty clothes, our bodies had gravitated toward each other's in the night despite the layers of blankets between us. His arm was draped across me, and my cheek rested against his chest, above his heart. His breath stirred my hair, surrounding me with his unique and intoxicating scent.

For three years, I'd wanted exactly this, and now, I had it—except I didn't, not really, because this was nothing more than survival, just two operatives sharing heat to avoid hypothermia.

His breathing shifted from the deep cadence of sleep, telling me he'd woken. I kept my own breathing steady, feigning unconsciousness, even as his body went rigid and the arm draped across me turned to granite.

The silence stretched between us—both of us awake, though I continued pretending otherwise—while his heartbeat raced faster than it should for someone just waking. Then he moved, extracting himself from me and the bed with the kind of caution usually reserved for disarming explosives, the mattress shifting as his weight left it and cold air rushing in where his warmth had been.

I listened as he crossed to the hearth and heard the scrape of the poker against stone. When the flames caught and grew, I sat up and brushed my tangled hair from my face.

"Morning," he muttered without turning to look at me.

"Morning," I responded in an equally cold tone.

I swung my legs out of bed, and my feet hit the floor, frigid even with my socks on, making me regret leaving the blankets. I tried to smooth my pants that were creased beyond salvation and untwist my black shirt from around my torso, but both were a lost cause.

"Bathroom's through there," he said. "You can go first."

I escaped through the door into a massive space that held a claw-foot tub that belonged in a museum and pipes that groaned when I turned the tap. The mirror above the sink showed me how rough I looked. There were dark circles beneath my eyes, and my hair was a nightmare of tangles. The water that sputtered from the tap smelled faintly of iron, but I splashed it on my face anyway, then finger-combed my hair into submission while trying not to think about how Tag had pulled away from me like I carried something contagious.

When I emerged, he took his turn without meeting my eyes. I used the time to fold the blankets and arrange them on the bed with their edges aligned—anything to occupy my hands, to avoid thinking about how different this morning was from what I'd conjured during the long nights when I allowed myself to imagine being in Tag's arms. Rather than sleeping, I dreamed of his naked body against mine, him inside me in a way no man had ever been before.

Understanding how inappropriate those thoughts had been didn't lessen the hurt of his inability to look at me.

The fire he'd rebuilt barely reached the corners of the room, and outside, wind whistled through gaps in the window frames.

When he finally emerged from the bathroom, he avoided my gaze completely, walking straight out of the room without a word and leaving me no choice but to grab my tablet and follow.

Our footsteps echoed as we descended the main staircase, passing portraits of generations of Cavendishes. Tag led with purposeful distance while I trailed behind, both of us maintaining an invisible barrier as carefully as if it were made of glass.

When we reached the bottom, he finally acknowledged my presence. "The kitchen should be this way," he said, veering left.

We continued through the great hall, where soaring ceilings were crossed with massive wooden beams above a table long enough to seat fifty people. Faded tapestries depicting hunts and battles covered the stone walls, flanking a fireplace large enough to roast an ox. The air in the room tasted of dust and age, with an underlying dampness that probably never diminished.

The kitchen, when we found it, was a mix of medieval bones and Victorian updates. Another enormous table, with scarred wood that had seen generations of meal preparation and a surface marked with knife scores and burns, dominated the center. Copper pots hung from iron hooks, green with verdigris at the joints. Against the far wall stood something I'd never encountered outside of BBC period dramas.

"Is that an AGA?" I asked, drawn to the massive cast-iron range radiating heat like a benevolent dragon.

"Old one, but functional." The hinges squealed in protest when Tag opened one of its heavy doors and checked inside. "While terribly inefficient in the way it burns oil continuously, it provides a cooking surface and heats the kitchen, making this the warmest room in the castle right now."

I held my hands toward it, and my fingers tingled as circulation returned.

"Wait here. I'll bring everything in from the SUV."

Rather than respond that I was capable of helping, I followed closely at his heels.

He scowled but didn't speak as we hauled the bags inside, then unpacked those meant for the kitchen. While Tag carried those containing clothing and incidentals upstairs, I filled a kettle from the tap that coughed and sputtered like the one upstairs had before flowing steadily. I set it on the AGA's hot plate, where it hissed, then found china cups, chipped but clean, in a cupboard and grabbed two tea bags that sat on the table, from those unpacked but not yet put away.

When Tag returned, he adjusted the dial of a radio whose plastic casing was yellowed with age. It crackled, then came to life on the counter, and a voice emerged through the static.

"As the onslaught of inclement weather strengthens over the North Sea, authorities warn of a potentially historic event. Coastal areas should prepare for extended power outages. All emergency services are currently suspended."

"It's getting worse rather than better," I said as rain lashed against the windows with enough force to make the old glass rattle in the frames.

"Significantly. Which means we could be here longer than anticipated."

I watched him remove the tea bag from his cup, place it in a spoon, and carry it over to a rubbish bin, all without as much as a glance in my direction. "I'll see if I can locate the heating system. In the meantime, you should ensure we have adequate water if the pipes freeze."

Before he could leave the room, a knock at the door made us both reach for our weapons—my hand found the grip of my Glock at my hip while Tag's went to the knife at his belt.

"Expecting anyone?" I asked.

"While I advised against it, Renegade mentioned the caretaker and his wife might try to make their way here this morning," he said, opening the heavy door. It groaned on hinges that probably predated the Industrial Revolution.

The couple on the doorstep looked like they'd stepped from a Highland romance novel with their weather-worn faces that had seen decades of Scottish gales, practical layered clothing, and the sturdy builds that came from lifetimes of physical work.

Beneath her knit hat, the woman's gray hair was pulled into a no-nonsense bun, and the man wore a tweed cap that did little to shield him from the raging downpour they'd come through.

"Mr. MacTaggert?" The woman's voice carried the musical cadence of the Scots, all soft consonants and rolled Rs. "I'm Mrs. MacLeod. This is my husband. Mr. Cavendish rang and said you'd need looking after."

"Please, come in." Tag stepped aside. "This is Ms. Nassar."

"Call me Leila," I said, moving to shake her hand.

The woman's keen eyes took in everything—our rumpled clothes, the intentional space between us, and the tension thick enough to cut with one of the swords decorating the walls. "You've found the kitchen, then. Good." The basket she handed to me held fresh bread, milk in a glass bottle, eggs with bits of straw stuck to them, and a container of homemade soup that smelled delicious.

"Let me show you what's what," her husband said, motioning for us to follow.

The tour he led us on revealed how little of the castle was habitable. As Renegade had mentioned, the east wing, where we'd slept, had heat, mostly, though Mrs. MacLeod warned that the radiators were temperamental and liked to clang in the night "like the devil himself was trapped in the pipes."

The west wing, she said, had been closed for the winter. When I peeked into one of the rooms, I saw the furniture was shrouded in dust sheets and the air was so cold my breath misted.

Mr. MacLeod stepped around me and pulled the door shut. "Best to keep this locked up tight. The west tower especially—it's not just the cold, you understand.

Structural concerns." He tapped the doorframe. "We wouldn't want either of you taking a tumble."

Tag nodded. "Understood."

The south tower was "best avoided unless you fancy falling through rotted floors," though Mr. MacLeod mentioned that his grandfather had hidden whiskey up there during the war and some might be there if we were so inclined.

"You can get to the old cellars through here," Mrs. MacLeod said, pointing to a door after we returned to the kitchen.

"Dangerous place, that," her husband added. "There's a storage area I'll show you, but don't be goin' beyond it." He shuddered. "My da lost a cousin down there in the fifties when it caved in. We've blocked most of it off, but you never know with these old places. I'd avoid them entirely if I were you."

"I'd like to take a look at the generator," Tag said.

"Aye, it's this way."

The door creaked open, and we made our way down the steep stone steps.

"It runs on diesel, and you've got maybe a week's worth if you're conservative. It'll power the essential circuits like the lights, refrigeration, and water pump.

The heating system has a separate tank that's fueled by oil, but can be unpredictable. Some radiators work, others don't. The ones that do might stop without warning. That's castle living for you," he said, chuckling.

He crouched down and ran his hand along the machine with the familiarity of someone who'd done this maintenance for years. "Been acting up more than usual this winter. Let me have a look while I'm here—see if I can't coax a bit more reliability out of the old girl."

Tag and I exchanged glances as Mr. MacLeod opened a panel and peered inside, making thoughtful humming noises.

"These old systems…I'll do what I can, but no promises. Might run smooth, might give you trouble. Hard to say."

"Appreciate you taking a look," Tag said.

"Aye, well." After a few minutes of looking at it versus doing anything, Mr. MacLeod straightened and wiped his hands on his trousers, though they didn't appear dirty. "Best I can do for now."

The supply stores were better stocked than expected, with candles by the box, torches with batteries that

Mrs. MacLeod warned might or might not work, and a military-surplus first-aid kit.

There was a shelf of canned goods with faded labels, likely older than me, but according to Mrs. MacLeod, they were *probably* still edible.

She led us upstairs, with her husband trailing behind us. "The roads will be impassable by tonight. We'll check on you when we can, but…" Her eyes moved between Tag and me with the kind of knowing look that made me wonder what she saw. "I'm thinking you'll want your privacy."

Tag asked a few more questions about security and who else had access to the property.

"You mentioned the area beyond the storeroom. Where does it lead?" I asked.

"Rumor is that you can access the old tunnels," Mr. MacLeod said almost dismissively, waving a gnarled hand. "It's Jacobite nonsense, if you ask me. My da said they were used to hide the Bonnie Prince's supporters. Some even tell stories about treasure hidden down there." He leveled a gaze at both of us. "You'd be wise to heed my warning about the danger."

I filed that information away, catching Tag doing the same. Our eyes met briefly—we'd be checking those tunnels at the first opportunity.

Mr. MacLeod pulled on his coat and checked his watch. "I'll need to be getting on. I've got two other properties to check before the roads become completely impassable."

Mrs. MacLeod was repacking her basket, adding a few items from the castle's stores. "There's a cottage on the grounds—the old gamekeeper's lodge. We've been using it when we come up to tend the place. I'll be just a short walk away if you need anything."

"That's not necessary—" I said, but she waved me off.

"Nonsense. You're Mr. Cavendish's guests, and I'll not have it said we left you to freeze in a drafty castle without proper guidance. Besides"—her eyes moved between Tag and me with that knowing look—"you'll want someone nearby who knows which pipes are likely to burst and where the spare candles are kept."

Her husband pulled his cap lower against the wind that howled through the door he'd cracked open. "Ring us if you need anything urgent. Though service is dodgy in weather like this." He nodded to Tag, then to me. "You'll be safe enough here as long as you remember what I said about those closed-off areas."

"We will," Tag assured him.

Mrs. MacLeod busied herself at the AGA, setting a pot to simmer as the Land Rover her husband drove disappeared down the drive.

"That'll be ready for your supper," she said, jotting a number on a piece of paper on the counter. "The gamekeeper's cottage has an old landline that still works when mobiles don't. Like Fergus said, ring if you need anything."

After she left, bundling herself against the weather and promising to return as soon as she could, the silence returned—heavier than before. With only two of us in the kitchen, it seemed smaller, and the AGA's warmth felt almost oppressive.

Tag refilled our teacups, and we sat at the scarred wooden table. "What happened after you left Syria?" he blurted.

The question stunned me. Where did I even start? I wrapped my hands around the warm china, grateful for something to hold.

"It makes more sense to tell you why I was there in the first place. What I was investigating."

His eyes scrunched, but he nodded.

"When Idris died, I received a letter from him." I turned away, not wanting to see his reaction. "It contained information about what he was working on." I took a deep breath and let it out slowly. I'd never admitted this aloud to anyone, and it was harder than I'd anticipated. Especially to Tag. "Project Labyrinth."

I heard his sharp intake of breath, but didn't pause long enough for him to speak.

"I also received an access code for encrypted files he left for me. They mentioned code names—Chimera, Janus, and someone called the Architect. There's more, but I've not been able to decipher the majority of it."

"Leila?"

My eyes met his.

"Are you saying this is why Idris died?"

I nodded, unable to speak.

"Why didn't you tell me? I could have—" He stopped himself, and I didn't interrupt. "I wish you would've trusted me," he added so quietly I almost couldn't hear him.

"For a long time, I didn't know who to trust, but it was more than that. What he was involved in, the information he left in my care, got him killed. It was one thing to risk my own life. Another thing to put other people in danger."

"But, why…?" He shook his head as though he figured out the answer before he asked the question. His eyes bored into mine. "This was the reason you were so determined to join Unit 23."

"Yes."

"Does Typhon know about the letter?"

"He does not." I couldn't gauge his reaction well enough to determine whether that bothered or relieved him.

"Since then, I've followed every lead, every clue. It's why I spent so much time in Damascus and how I figured out Eric Weber was an alias Fallon Wallace used, then eventually, that she was Chimera."

"You said there's more?"

"Yes, but beyond anything I can break."

"I sense there's a lot you're not saying."

He was right, but even now, I couldn't confess that Idris had never intended for me to take on the investigation. His letter had been very clear. *Take all of this to Niall MacTaggert. You can trust him.*

I'd chosen not to for reasons I couldn't explain. That revelation would have to wait until I was ready for his reaction—which might be never.

"Do you think this is why you're being followed?" he asked when I didn't respond.

"Maybe." I shrugged. "But why after all this time?"

"It could have something to do with Fallon Wallace's death. That you connected her to Weber and Chimera."

"It's one theory."

"What about the Architect? Any theories about that?" he asked.

"It could be McLaren. Or Orlov."

He nodded. "Neither of which can confirm or deny it at this point. One is dead, and one might as well be." He sipped his tea. "What really happened in Syria?"

I hated how easily he could read me. Or knew me. Yes, there'd been a coup, but that wasn't the only reason I'd requested extraction.

"I was able to piece together something else in Idris' files that I hadn't understood until then. I received intel about a mole within MI6. Someone on the inside who'd been feeding information to the Labyrinth network."

"You 'received intel.' Let me guess, from Kestrel?"

My gaze remained steady on his, but I didn't confirm or deny what he'd said. He knew I wouldn't. Not yet anyway.

"I made Typhon aware of it during my debrief in Glasgow, which is why I disappeared the next day."

His jaw tightened, and he scowled. "There are times I hate that *sonuvabitch*."

"I'll admit to occasionally feeling the same way."

"Go on. Forgive my interruption."

"He arranged for a new location and complete blackout. That's when Viper took over as my handler."

His eyes widened. "The chief of MI6 became your handler?"

"It made sense, given the circumstances. If there was a mole, we needed to keep the circle as small as possible." I stood, too restless to sit. "We spent several days going through everything. Cross-referencing communications, tracking patterns, building a profile."

"And?"

"We narrowed it down to a handful of possibilities." I set my cup on the counter. "Eventually, we zeroed in on one name. Malcolm Bennett."

Recognition flickered across his face.

"He was a mid-level analyst with a cryptography background," I continued. "And had access to exactly the kind of information that had been leaked."

Tag stood and paced across the room. "What happened next?"

"Viper sent him to work with Con and Lex to see if he'd make a move." I stood by the window, studying the sleet as it streaked down the glass. "Then the lab exploded, and Bennett and McLaren died. At least we think that's what happened. As I'm sure you know, her body was never found."

Tag stilled. "You think she's alive."

"I do." I chose my next words judiciously. "I told you I thought either she or Orlov could be 'the Architect.'"

"Go on."

"There were certain things about him or her, specific skill sets, operational patterns. After the explosion, when similar patterns emerged through fresh intel, I figured it couldn't be Orlov. The next best guess was McLaren."

Tag's eyes narrowed. "That's a significant leap."

"It is. But when I began pulling threads, everything fell into place." I moved to retrieve my tablet from where I'd left it on the counter. "After her supposed death, I went through the Syrian intel again systematically and narrowed it into four categories."

I pulled up the files and turned the screen toward him. "First, the communications. Encrypted channels between Damascus, Cyprus, and somewhere in Scotland. The coding was complex, but once I broke it down, I discovered the messages use technical terminology she coined. Specific phrase constructions. Even the way she structures her arguments—it's like hearing someone's voice in their writing."

Tag moved to stand next to me and studied the screen. "That's not proof."

"No, it's not. Second, the financial trail. I found transfers also through Cyprus but in Malta too. Small amounts, nothing that would trigger standard monitoring protocols, but they aggregate over time."

I swiped to the next file. "Third, operational patterns. Cells we thought were eliminated are active again. Different leadership on the surface, but the same infrastructure, same tradecraft. And fourth, technical signatures. Only two people ever understood the AIWS technology at this level—Orlov and her."

"And Lex," he added.

"Yes, Lex neutralized the interface at Orlov's lab, but she learned from McLaren's and Orlov's work. She didn't pioneer it."

He didn't speak for several seconds. "The people following you in London. They don't want to kill you. At least not yet. They want to know how much you know."

I closed the tablet. "I agree."

"So we act on the assumption that they know you're onto them."

"Yes. And, soon enough, they'll know I'm with you. If they don't already."

Tag didn't react. People like him—myself included—never did. We couldn't. If we spent all our time looking over our shoulder, we'd sign our own death warrant.

"It could be someone else who learned from McLaren," Tag said, his shoulders tense.

"Yes." I crossed my arms. "Or it could be her. Whoever this is has been cautiously acquiring resources, technology, and personnel.

"If she's alive, then is the supposition that she's trying to recreate what was destroyed in the explosion?"

"No idea. Although I don't think she's Janus—the mastermind. I found references to her communicating with someone about moving into phase two. She isn't calling the shots."

"There's something else," Tag said. "Sullivan Rivers traced Tower-Meridian's shipments out of Tees, then through Felixstowe. The working theory is that AIWS components are being moved through ancient tunnel networks. If they exist."

I considered it. "It makes sense. The very definition of Labyrinth is a complicated and irregular network of passages."

"Not terribly clever on their part," he muttered.

"They have far bigger things on their minds," I agreed.

Tag's gaze fixed on something beyond the window. "You ran again yesterday. Why?"

"Viper said they were getting closer. Bolder." I sank into the chair. "She arranged for an MI6 extraction team, but then I received word that hostile forces were moving in. I couldn't wait."

"Kestrel again." He approached the table, pulled one of the chairs out, and motioned for me to sit. After I had, he pulled the other chair closer to mine. "I have another question, and this time, I want you to answer me honestly."

I waited, biting my lip.

"Leila, did you want me to find you?"

Of everything he could've asked, that question might be the hardest for me to answer. Yes, I had. Maybe because I was tired of being on my own. Maybe I missed Idris so much and Tag was the closest connection I had to him.

He spoke before I did. "Three years ago, I promised your brother I'd look after you. That promise doesn't have an expiration date. You know that, don't you?"

It was as though he'd read my mind. "I do."

"What you aren't sure of yet is how much you can trust me with."

"I…" I shook my head.

"It's okay, Leila. Either way, you're stuck with me." He winked, and for the first time since our conversation began, I smiled.

"He'd be disappointed in how little I've accomplished. Months of investigation, and I'm no closer to understanding the full scope of Project Labyrinth."

"You confirmed Bennett was dirty. You found evidence suggesting McLaren is alive. That's not nothing."

"It's not enough."

"It's a start." He took my hand in his. "And you're not working alone anymore." For a moment, his thumb brushed across my knuckles, and something flickered in his eyes—something warm and unguarded. Then, as if catching himself, he jerked his hand away and stood abruptly.

Before I could react, Tag's mobile chimed. He glanced at the screen, then set it on the table between us and put it on speaker.

"Hey, Renegade."

"Hiya, boss. How's the family castle treating you? Fair warning—the plumbing screams like a banshee and the west tower's been trying to fall down for thirty years or more."

Despite everything, Tag's mouth quirked. "You're underselling the place's ambiance. We've got heat in about half the rooms and a generator that might last the week if we're lucky."

"Sounds about right. The chimney in the library smokes if the wind is from the north, and whatever you do, don't trust the third step from the top on the servants' stairs. How's Nightingale? Is she surviving the Dunravin hospitality?"

Tag's eyes flicked to me. "She's…adapting. Any updates?"

"The storm is getting worse. The news outlets are calling it a once-in-a-generation event. You're looking at a week minimum, possibly longer. Several roads are already compromised—some are completely washed out. Even helicopter extraction would be dicey until this passes, since winds are gusting at ninety miles per hour."

"Copy that," Tag said before ending the call.

A week. Possibly longer? How in the hell would I get through it?

Silence stretched between us, broken only by the rattling windows and the rain hammering stone. Tag picked up his mug and set it in the sink. His back was to me, but I could see how his knuckles had turned white with how hard he gripped the edge of the counter.

"We need to establish clear boundaries. Professional boundaries."

He turned to face me, but his eyes focused some-where over my shoulder. "Last night, sharing the bed—that was about survival, nothing more. It can't happen again. I'll take the room across the hall tonight. We should set up a schedule so we're not…" His jaw tightened. "So we're not in each other's way unnecessarily. We'll need to conserve fuel for the generator anyway, so coordinating our movements makes sense."

The clinical tone in his voice, the way he couldn't even look at me—as if this morning when we'd woken tangled together meant nothing, as if taking my hand moments ago hadn't happened—told me everything I needed to know about where I stood with him.

"Sorry, I need to…" I pushed away from the table and headed for the stairs, needing distance before I said more I'd regret. Not about Idris. About him and how much it hurt that he was planning our week like we were strangers who needed to avoid each other.

My emotions were raw enough from all I'd confessed. I couldn't deal with more right now. I needed space. Time to think. Maybe confiding in him was a mistake. One of the biggest of my life.

"Leila, wait—"

I took the stairs two at a time, but partway up, my foot caught the edge of a worn step. The stone crumbled under my boot. I pitched forward, hands scrambling for the banister that was too far to reach. The momentum carried me sideways toward the steep drop.

My shoulder hit the steps, then my hip scraped against the wall. The world spun. Four steps, five—

Strong arms caught me, and Tag's body absorbed my impact as we both continued falling. He'd managed to turn us so his back took the brunt of it. His arms locked around me as we slid to a stop at the landing.

"Christ, Leila." His voice was rough against my ear, his chest heaving beneath me. "Are you hurt?"

I couldn't respond. Not because of pain—though my shoulder throbbed and my hip would definitely bruise—but because of how tightly he held me. Like I might disappear. Like he actually cared.

His hands moved over me, checking for injuries. "Your shoulder—"

"I'm fine." My voice came out shakier than intended.

"You could have broken your neck." His words were fierce, almost angry, but his arms didn't loosen. If anything, they tightened. "These stairs are ancient—"

"I said I'm fine."

We were sprawled on the floor, with me on top of him. His heartbeat hammered against my chest, and his hands stilled on my waist. When I lifted my head, he looked like he was in shock.

"You caught me," I said stupidly.

"Always." The unguarded word came out raw, and his hand moved to my face. His thumb brushed along my cheekbone where I'd scraped it against the wall. "I'll always catch you."

"Tag," I whispered.

Something shifted in his eyes—a decision made in an instant. His hand slid into my hair, and he pulled me closer, or maybe I was the one to do it, then again, perhaps we met in the middle. But his mouth found mine, and three years of wanting exploded between us.

The kiss wasn't gentle. It was frantic and impassioned, with everything we'd been denying poured into it. His other arm wrapped around my waist, holding me against him as his mouth devoured mine. My hands gripped his shoulders as I kissed him with equal fervor.

When we finally broke apart, I stared into his eyes that were black with desire. For a heartbeat, the truth lay bare between us, then reality crashed in. His walls rebuilt, and I saw the instant he remembered all the reasons why this couldn't happen. His hands dropped away after he helped me sit up.

"We should—" His voice was hoarse. He cleared his throat, tried again. "We should, um, make sure you're okay."

"I'm not," I whispered.

His eyes scrunched like he wasn't sure if I meant literally, but rather than move away, he gathered me in his arms so my cheek rested against his chest, like it had when we woke this morning.

When he leaned away and cupped my face, I prayed he'd kiss me again, but he didn't. He rested his forehead against mine and whispered words that broke my heart.

"We can't do this."

4

Tag

"We can't do this."

Leila's defensive wall slid into place as though she'd learned how best to protect herself from disappointment when my harsh words escaped before I could stop them.

Her body was warm despite the cold floor beneath us, and her pulse raced under my hand. The taste of honey, heat, and denied wanting lingered on my lips. Our kiss had been everything I imagined and more, which was exactly why it could never happen again.

"I—" She stopped herself, then shifted away from me entirely. "Are you hurt?" she asked. "Your back took most of the impact."

"I'm fine." The lie came automatically, though my spine screamed in protest where it had connected with the stone surface. But the physical pain was manageable. What I'd done—kissing her like a man starved, pulling her against me like I had any right to—that was the real damage.

After helping her stand, my hands moved over her body, checking the shoulder that had hit the wall and the hip where her clothes had torn. Even through the fabric, I could feel her strength and the toned muscles that came from years of training. She tolerated my inspection for a few seconds before withdrawing.

"I need to clean up." Her jaw was tight as she spoke, her words so measured they could have been about ops protocol or mission goals. Without waiting for a response, she turned and headed up the stairs, moving far slower than before and with the kind of dignity that made my chest constrict.

I remained at the bottom, gripping the banister until the wood groaned under my hands. My knuckles went white, then whiter still, as I fought the urge to follow her. To explain. To apologize. And God help me, to kiss her again.

Christ. What had I been thinking?

The answer was simple. I hadn't been. I'd spent years keeping her at arm's length, calling her "kid" to remind us both of what she was to me—Idris' sister. That familiar refrain had kept me in check through countless missions and all the times she'd gazed at me with something more than respect.

It was more than her being my dead asset's sister who I promised to protect. Leila was the kind of woman I couldn't just walk away from without a backward glance. She'd need more, want more, and deserved more. None of which I could give her.

But the memory of her response threatened to shred every rational argument I'd built. She'd kissed me like she was waiting for it. Like she'd been thinking about it for as long as I had. The sound she'd made when I deepened the kiss, the way her fingers had tangled in my hair, the way her body had melted against mine—

No. I couldn't think about that. I wouldn't allow myself to.

I forced myself to move, to climb the stairs on unsteady legs. I owed her a proper explanation, not the harsh rejection I'd just thrown at her, but the truth about why what had happened, incredible as it had been, could never again.

I searched the castle's maze of rooms, finally finding her in the second-level library twenty minutes later. She stood at one of the tall windows, watching the maelstrom rage against the glass. The light, more like dusk than morning, caught her profile—her defined cheekbones and the way her hair, now freed, fell in waves

past her shoulders. She'd changed into other clothes—
black leggings that outlined legs I shouldn't notice and
an oversized jumper that made her look both younger
and impossibly alluring. The bruise blooming on her
cheekbone from the fall made protective instincts rise
in my chest.

The room itself seemed to mock me with its floor-
to-ceiling shelves filled with leather-bound volumes, a
fire crackling in the massive hearth, and the relentless
rain that continued falling. It was the kind of romantic
setting found in the novels my sister would talk about,
where the brooding lord finally confessed his feelings to the governess or whoever. Except this wasn't a
romance novel, and I wasn't about to confess anything
except why we couldn't be together.

"Leila, we need to talk. There are things you
should know—"

When she turned to face me, the cool assessment in
her eyes stopped me. Gone was any trace of the woman
who'd kissed me less than half an hour ago. This was
Special Agent Nassar, code name Nightingale, regarding me with the same detachment she might show a
problematic asset. But I knew her well enough to
see the hurt beneath the surface, the way her full lips

pressed together, and the tension that had settled in her shoulders.

"I get it, Tag. I'm a responsibility. Nothing more."

"That isn't true, and while I know it sounds trite, in this case, it isn't you, Leila. It's me."

"It isn't necessary to explain," she said, stepping away from the window and putting the heavy oak reading table between us like a battle line. The movement highlighted her grace and the way she carried herself with the confidence of someone who knew exactly what her body was capable of.

"My mother and father…" I cleared my throat when my words felt like glass in my throat. I'd never told anyone the entire story, not even Con, Ash, or Gus. Although they'd witnessed most of it firsthand. "They met at university in Edinburgh. My mum was studying art history, my dad economics. According to my aunt, they couldn't keep their hands off each other. They had the kind of passion that singed everything in its path."

Her brow furrowed, but she didn't speak.

"They married within six months of meeting. Then had me within the year. My brother was born two years later, and my sister eighteen months after that. Sometime between the wedding and my fifth birthday, their passionate love turned poisonous." I moved to the hearth. I needed something to do with my hands, so I added wood to the dying flames. The logs, damp from the humidity, hissed as they caught. "Every day became a new battle. Breakfast was a minefield of passive aggression, while dinner was open warfare. They knew exactly how to wound each other. They'd spent years refining their aim."

The blaze caught properly, but the warmth did nothing to ease the chill that had settled in my chest from the memories.

"The affairs began when I was seven. First, my dad had one with his secretary, then my mum with her tennis instructor. They didn't even try to hide them from us by the end. When she'd come home with her lipstick smudged, smelling of another man's cologne, my father would pour himself another whiskey. He'd disappear for entire weekends with women half his age while she entertained her lovers in our home." I turned to face Leila, forcing myself to meet her gaze. "They stayed together out of spite, I think. Wanting to see who could hurt the other more, to see who would break first. They used us—my siblings and me—as weapons in their war. We became their leverage, their ammunition."

"Tag…" Leila's voice was soft, comforting, but I couldn't let myself get lost in it.

"When I was sixteen, my mum finally left. We—my brother, sister, and I—came home from boarding school for a long weekend holiday to find her things missing. She'd taken everything that was hers, the paintings she'd inherited from her grandparents, the silver, even the photo albums with our baby pictures. But she left us. Her children. We haven't seen her since."

The silence between us was broken only by the raging weather outside.

"We found our father in the drawing room. God only knew how long he'd been drunk. By the looks of it, it had been days."

Leila's eyes filled with tears. Of pity no doubt, but I'd begun this story, and I had to finish it.

"That same day, standing in what was left of our home, I made a decision. I vowed I would never marry, never enter into something that could become that toxic, never give someone the power to destroy me the way they destroyed each other."

"You chose to never let anyone close." Her voice was quiet, understanding rather than questioning.

"I chose to accept that love wasn't real. Passion was. But in the end, it always morphed into destruction waiting to happen. I'm thirty-four, Leila, and I've never had a relationship last longer than a weekend. That's not by accident—it's by design."

Her hands gripped the edge of the table. "Why are you telling me this?"

"Because you're twenty-two. You're brilliant and capable and fierce. You have your whole life ahead of you, a chance at something real with someone who can give you what you deserve. You shouldn't waste your time on someone who's already decided how this ends. On someone who witnessed love turn malignant and decided the only winning move was not to play."

The anger that flashed across her face was breathtaking. When she pushed away from the table, the light caught the gold flecks in her hazel eyes, turning them molten.

"You don't get to decide what I should or shouldn't waste my time on."

"Leila—"

"No." She was close enough now that I could see every detail—the way her chest rose and fell, the flush on her cheeks, the determined set of her beautiful mouth. "You don't get to kiss me the way you did, then tell me it's for my own good that it won't happen again."

"That kiss was my fault. I lost control, and no, it will not happen again."

She stared at me for several heartbeats before her expression shifted. "Right. Your fault. Your control. Your decision." Each step was measured and deliberate as she moved toward the door. "Message received, Tag. Loud and clear. You've decided I'm too young, too innocent, too *whatever* to know what I want. Like you've done since the day you met me."

"That's not—"

"Isn't it?" She paused at the doorway, but didn't turn around. "You've been calling me 'kid' since my brother died. Treating me like I might break, making decisions about what's best for me without ever asking what I want. I thought maybe…but no. You're right. This won't happen again."

She left, and I stood alone, certain that I'd done the right thing even as everything in me screamed that I was a fool. I remained motionless even as the memory of her kiss threatened to bring me to my knees.

I spent the next few hours pacing the downstairs library like a caged animal, trying to focus on the mission, Janus, AIWS—anything but the look on Leila's face when she'd stalked away.

She was right, of course. It had been exactly that long since I first yearned to know how her lips would feel beneath mine. I'd spent all that time treating her like she was a nineteen-year-old who'd entered the Unit 23 training facility with her brother's death fresh in her eyes. But what she didn't understand then or now was that staying away from her had nothing to do with age or innocence. It was about me being too damaged, too terrified of what we could become if I let myself care for her the way I wanted to.

The deluge continued its assault on the castle, with wind howling through gaps in the timeworn stones. Somewhere in the walls, pipes groaned and settled. The radiators clanged intermittently, and the whole place seemed alive, observing my misery with the judgment of centuries.

The sound of movement in the kitchen finally drew me from my self-imposed isolation. The sun had set, though the dark clouds made the distinction largely academic. The castle's electricity flickered intermittently, casting everything in unreliable light.

I found Leila at the AGA, stirring a pot. She'd tied her hair in a messy bun, and when she turned to face me, I had to force myself not to stare at the spot where my lips had been only hours ago.

"Are you hungry? Mrs. MacLeod's soup smells incredible."

The shift to civility was so smooth it gave me whiplash. She acted as if the last few hours—hell, the last day—hadn't happened at all. As if we hadn't kissed. As if I hadn't broken something between us that might never heal.

"Leila, about earlier—"

"Don't." She didn't look up from ladling soup into bowls. "There's nothing more to say."

She set the bowls on the table with the fresh bread Mrs. MacLeod had provided, then sat down. I took the chair across from her, noticing the bruise on her cheek had turned purple-black against her bronze skin. I had to fight the urge to reach across the table and touch it, to apologize for not catching her sooner, for not protecting her from the fall. And most of all, for not protecting her from me.

We ate in silence after that. Though the soup was rich and warming, I barely tasted it.

Every movement Leila made, every breath, reminded me of what I couldn't have. What I wouldn't allow myself to have. The way she tucked a strand of hair that had escaped her bun behind her ear, the way her throat moved when she swallowed, and the faint mark on her neck where my stubble had scraped against her skin during our kiss.

Christ. I couldn't do this. I pushed my chair from the table and stood. After cleaning the bowl and spoon, I left the kitchen and headed upstairs. Before I reached the doorway of the bedroom across the hall from hers, I saw her approaching.

"Don't do this. It's ridiculous for you to sleep elsewhere." Fatigue deepened her voice. "We can share a bed without…"

Without what? Without touching? Without wanting? Without remembering how exquisitely we'd fit together when we kissed?

"Okay," I said, following her into the bedroom that seemed smaller than it had this morning. The walls appeared closer, and the air felt heavier. We took turns in the bathroom, changing into sleep clothes with the door firmly closed between us. I pulled track pants and a sweatshirt on, trying not to think about her doing the same. When I emerged, she was already under the covers on the far side of the bed, turned away from the center.

I got in on my side, staying as close to the edge as physics would allow. The space between us might as well have been an ocean. Or maybe a minefield—it was dangerous to cross, potentially explosive. The mattress was old enough that it dipped slightly in the middle, trying to pull us together, but we both clung to our edges with grim determination.

I stared at the ceiling, hyperaware of her presence. Her breathing was uneven. She was awake, as I was, and both of us were lying there, pretending not to be.

The memory of the kiss haunted me. I couldn't forget the way she'd responded, like she'd been waiting for it as long as I had. Or the heat of her mouth, the softness of her full lips, and the way she'd fit against me like our bodies were made to be close.

Last night, we'd gravitated toward one another. Now, we fought that pull, clinging to our separate territories like our lives depended on it. Because maybe they did. Or at least, mine did.

The clock on the mantel chimed midnight. Then one. Then two. Then three. Still, I couldn't sleep. Every time she shifted, perhaps trying to find a comfortable position, it sent desire pulsing through me. If only she'd face me. Then I wouldn't—couldn't—resist her. But she didn't. And it was the longest night of my life.

5

Nightingale

The day broke, gray and violent. Outside, the storm raged with renewed fury. I hadn't slept, and I doubted Tag had, either. We moved around each other with exhausted wariness, preparing a breakfast of tea and yesterday's bread toasted on the AGA. My eyes burned from fighting tears all night, and my body ached from clinging to the edge of the mattress.

In the harsh morning light, the exhaustion etched on Tag's face—circles under his eyes, the rigid set of his jaw—was evident. Even fatigued, he was devastating. I hated that I noticed every detail about the man—the way his hair fell across his forehead as he buttered his toast, making sure every corner was covered equally. Even after his rejection, after his confession designed to push me away, I wanted him.

"We should explore the tunnels." His voice was rough. "Map them while we're here."

"Agreed," I said, grateful for action, for purpose, for anything that wasn't sitting in this kitchen, pretending

I hadn't spent the entire night fighting the urge to turn to him.

After we'd gathered what we'd need. I checked my gun and chambered a round.

Tag did the same with his, then we descended onto the stone steps. Our lights carved through the shadows as we continued farther down to the tunnel's concealed entrance.

Working together despite the tension between us, we mapped the passages systematically. Tag did rough sketches while I photographed every intersection, every marker, every architectural detail that might matter.

"This is eighteenth century," I said, running my hand along a section of stonework, needing to fill the quiet with something safe, something that wasn't about us. My fingers found the mason's marks, reading them like braille. "See these chisel patterns? They match what I've seen in books on Jacobite construction methods."

I moved to another section, training my torch on what lay ahead. "But this section is Victorian—see the different mortar? They expanded it, probably during the Highland Clearances, when families were forced from their homes."

"You know your Scottish history," Tag said, and there was something in his voice—surprise? Maybe even approval? I couldn't tell without glancing at him, and I wouldn't let myself.

"My mother was fascinated by it. Before she met my father, she spent a year at the University of Edinburgh, studying the Jacobite period. She used to tell Idris and me stories about the clans, battles, and betrayals. I think she treasured the romance of it all—doomed causes and noble sacrifices."

When Tag didn't respond, I wondered if he'd even heard me.

Rather than follow his lead, I went deeper, finding evidence of modifications from the early twentieth century—concrete reinforcements and metal brackets for long-dead electrical systems.

"It goes deeper than we thought," Tag said, studying the branching passages.

"My guess is they're part of an elaborate network," I agreed, forcing myself to focus on the meaning rather than how close he stood and how his presence warmed the air around him in this frigid place. "Look how they connect—multiple routes, redundancies. You could move through here even if one section collapsed.

Whoever designed this was planning for siege conditions, long-term hiding, maybe even counterattack."

We continued through passages that extended far beyond what any single castle would need for escape. We found debris left over centuries—rusted tools, fragments of crates, provisions turned to dust. Evidence of the tunnels' use during various conflicts, including a button from a military uniform that was tarnished beyond identification, and a child's wooden toy, left behind in some long-ago flight.

"We need to check that area," I said, shining my torch down a tunnel that narrowed significantly. "It might lead to another section."

The space contracted gradually until we had to move in single file, then forced us to our hands and knees. I went first since I was significantly smaller in stature.

Halfway through the tightest section, I got hung up on a jutting edge. I tried to shift, to work myself free, but the angle was wrong. The rock had wedged against my shoulder blade, pinning me.

"I'm stuck." The words came out steadier than my hammering pulse suggested. I tried to slow my breathing but felt as though the walls were closing in on me.

"Don't panic. I'll get you free," said Tag from behind me.

"My shoulder's wedged. I can't—" I fought to keep my voice level even as claustrophobia clawed at my throat. "I can't move in either direction."

"Okay. I'm going to reach forward. Try to relax."

His hands were on my waist, and even through layers of clothing, his touch burned. How was it possible that after everything—after his rejection, his walls, his litany of reasons we couldn't be together—it felt like they belonged on my body?

"On three," he said through gritted teeth. "Try to adjust your shoulders while I pull. One, two—"

He pulled as I twisted, and I was free, tumbling into him. We landed in a heap where the tunnel was wider. We were both breathing hard as my body pressed against his. Neither of us moved for several seconds, and I could feel his rapid heartbeat pound against my spine. His arms were wrapped around me, and all it would take to find his mouth was for me to turn my head. Instead, I scrambled off him like he was burning me, because in a way, he was.

We stood, both pretending nothing had happened. Because really, nothing had.

"It looks like there's another way in," Tag said, motioning to our left.

The chamber I followed him into was more of a natural cave than anywhere else we'd entered. Tool marks marred the walls, old iron brackets had been installed to hold torches, and two wooden benches showed wear from use. Had it been a hiding place? A meeting room? My imagination ran wild as I pictured what had gone on in Scotland's violent past.

"This is incredible," I said, examining the masonry, forcing myself to focus on the historical significance rather than on the man who made concentrating on anything other than him nearly impossible. "Jacobite era, definitely. They must have used this during the uprising. Look—" I traced carved initials on the wall. "Someone left their mark. IR 1746. The year of Culloden."

"The last stand," Tag said quietly. "According to history books, after that, the Highland way of life was systematically destroyed."

We took a different way out that proved to be more torturous. At one point, I had to press against Tag to navigate a particularly tight turn, and he went rigid behind me.

When we finally emerged into the main undercroft, we were both shaking—from the plummeting temperatures, exhaustion, and for me, from the effort of maintaining impossible boundaries when every instinct demanded I drop them.

"We should brief Typhon on what we found," I said, brushing dust from my clothes.

"Agreed. I'll handle it. You should rest."

"I'm fine."

He muttered something under his breath that I'd be damned before I'd ask him to repeat it.

As we climbed back into the kitchen, the throbbing in my shoulder, where it had caught in the tunnel, got worse. Without thinking, I rubbed at it, trying to ease the ache. I saw Tag's hand move toward me, but I stepped away before he could touch me. I couldn't bear his comfort, not when it came with such strict limits. Not when I knew he'd be gentle, then call me "kid" in the next breath.

"I'm fine," I repeated, moving to peer out the window at nature's relentless assault. Trees bent over like supplicants before an angry god, and debris flew past like missiles. The North Sea was visible in the distance, a churning mass of gray and white with waves tall enough to swallow houses.

The afternoon dragged on with excruciating slowness. We'd eaten a quiet lunch of leftover soup from Mrs. MacLeod's provisions, and Tag had checked his mobile, but the signal was too weak to get through to either Typhon or Viper. I felt truly isolated now, cut off from Unit 23, MI6, London, and everything except each other and this crumbling castle.

Eventually, Tag suggested another exploration of the tunnels—something I was happy to do. Anything to avoid sitting in the same room, drowning in silence.

This time, we took a different branch, one that led toward what we calculated was the direction of the sea. The sound of our footsteps echoed as we descended deeper into the earth.

The tunnel here was different—rougher, more medieval. Some sections were so old the walls had worn smooth from countless hands touching them for guidance. I ran my fingers along them, sensing the history that had seeped into them. How many people had fled through here? How many secrets had these walls kept?

"When was the castle constructed?" I asked, examining the composition more closely.

"The original foundation dates back to the thirteenth century. These tunnels might have been here almost from the beginning," Tag responded.

We'd been working for perhaps an hour when we reached another chamber, this one partially collapsed. Rubble blocked most of the space, but there was a gap near the ceiling, where someone small might squeeze through. The debris appeared decades old. Tag called out from behind me as I moved closer to examine what looked like carved symbols on the far wall.

"Watch it, kid. That beam doesn't look stable."

Kid. I clenched my fists and jaw, and my brow furrowed. After the kiss that had shattered both of us, after spending the night clinging to opposite sides of the bed like our lives depended on it, after the way he'd held me after I was stuck in the tunnel—he still called me that.

Something inside me snapped. Years of frustration, of being diminished, of being seen as less than what I was—all boiled over in an instant.

I whirled on him, my torch beam catching his surprised expression. "Stop calling me that."

He blinked at my vehemence. "I didn't mean—"

"Stop treating me like I'm fragile. Like I'm something to protect and pat on the head." The words poured out, a flood I couldn't stop even if I'd wanted to. "You do it every single day. Every. Single. Fucking. Day. I've killed people, Tag. I've run ops that would make seasoned agents think twice. I survived alone for months in Syria, extracted assets from Tehran when everyone said it was impossible and decoded intelligence that saved dozens of lives. I've earned my place at Unit 23 ten times over. But you call me 'kid' like I'm someone who needs to be managed rather than trusted."

"That's not fair," he spat at me.

"Isn't it?" I stepped closer, fury overriding every instinct that told me not to. "You told me yesterday it wasn't about me being Idris' sister. That it was about you, about your past. Fine. I get that. But that doesn't change the fact that you treat me like I'm nineteen, like I'm that girl at her brother's funeral. I'm twenty-two years old. I speak five languages fluently, and I can kill a man sixteen different ways with my bare hands. I've infiltrated organizations that would execute me without hesitation if they knew who I really was. I'm not a child, Tag. I haven't been one for a very long time."

"I know that." His tone was low, seething.

"Do you? Because from where I'm standing, you see the teenager you and Typhon approached at the cemetery. The girl you promised to protect. Well, I don't need protecting, Tag. Not from missions, not from danger, and certainly not from you."

The hush that followed was deafening. Even the constant drip of water somewhere in the tunnels seemed to pause. Tag's eyes had gone almost black in the torchlight, and when he spoke, his voice was barely above a whisper.

"I don't see you as a kid." Each word dragged from him against his will, like he was confessing under torture. "That's the problem."

My breath caught, and the hair on my arms stood up. Understanding crashed through me—the walls weren't about dismissal. It was defense. He was trying to convince himself as much as me.

"Tag—"

"We should return to the main level." He stalked off, leaving me standing alone with my heart hammering.

I eventually followed, and when I emerged from the undercroft, the warmth I'd anticipated was nonexistent.

As if it were the proverbial straw breaking the camel's back, the generator wheezed, then died completely. The lights flickered off, leaving us in the gray twilight.

"The heat's given out," he said, checking the cooling radiators. "We'll have to rely on other ways to stay warm."

We built up the fire in the bedroom since it was the most contained space, but even with the flames roaring, the chilled air was bitter, seeping through the exterior and finding every gap in the windows where frost had formed on the inside of the glass.

Night fell early, the bad weather turning daylight to dusk by sixteen hundred hours. We ate dinner sitting as close as we could to the hearth—bread and cheese accompanied by a bottle of whiskey Tag had discovered in a cupboard. It was aged and smoky, and the burn of each sip spread warmth through my chest and limbs.

"We're going to freeze," I said as my breath clouded in the air despite sitting close to the fire.

Tag had been staring into the flames, but at my words, he glanced up. The light caught his features, casting shadows that emphasized the exhaustion on his face and the tension in his jaw. "We'll manage."

"No, we won't." I stood, decision made. "We need to share body heat, or we'll both be hypothermic by morning."

I saw him tense, saw the automatic rejection forming, but I cut him off.

"This isn't about *us*. It's about survival."

He was quiet for several seconds, then nodded once. "You're right."

We sat with our spines against the sofa, sharing the blankets we'd gathered from around the castle. At first, we maintained space between us, but the cold was relentless. Within minutes, we'd shifted closer, our bodies naturally seeking warmth.

His arm was behind me on the sofa, not quite touching but close enough for me to sense its presence. Heat radiated from him through our clothes.

"Better?" His tone was low and rough.

"Yes."

"Tell me about Idris when you were growing up," he said into the quiet. "What was he like as a brother?"

"He was…" I searched for words to capture someone so complex. "Protective. Brilliant. Infuriating." A smile tugged at my lips despite the ache in my chest.

"He taught me to pick locks when I was twelve. Mum and Dad were furious."

"Sounds like him." There was warmth in Tag's voice, real affection. "He talked about you constantly. Every mission, every dead drop, there'd be something about his little sister. How proud he was. How smart you were. How he worried about you."

"He talked about you too." I raised my chin and turned in his direction. "He said you were the most honorable man he'd ever met and that if anything happened to him, I could trust you with my life."

"He made me promise…"

"I know."

Tag shifted and dropped his arm from the sofa to rest around my shoulders.

I leaned into him, fitting myself against his side. His arm tightened, and he exhaled as tension left his body.

"He wanted me to be happy," I said quietly.

"He wanted you safe."

"From what? From living?" I leaned away enough to see his face. "Tag, I chose this life. I chose Unit 23. I chose to follow in his footsteps not because I had to, but because I wanted to. Every decision I've made has been mine. Not his. Not yours. *Mine.*"

"I know," he said as though the words hurt him to say. "God help me, I know."

We stayed like that for a long time, wrapped in blankets and each other's warmth. Neither of us suggested moving to the bed; we were nearer the heat where we were.

"Tag," I whispered.

"Yeah?"

"I wish you could see me differently. As a woman."

His hand found mine under the blankets, and he wove his fingers with mine. "I've always seen you as a woman."

His thumb moved against my palm, and my breathing went shallow.

"Leila." My name sounded like an oath.

I shifted an inch closer, but it was enough. Our cheeks touched, and he shuddered. His free hand came up to cup my face with heartbreaking gentleness.

"We shouldn't," he whispered, but his actions contradicted his words as he traced the line of my jaw.

I tilted my head toward his. "I know."

For an instant, we hovered there, lips barely an inch apart. Then, as if pulled by invisible strings, the space between us disappeared.

The kiss was nothing like the desperate collision on the stairs. This was slower and deeper. His hand tangled in my hair, holding me like I might disappear. Every line of my body fitted against his as we shifted lower, lying on the blankets beneath us.

The sound that came from low in his throat conveyed surrender. He rolled us so I was beneath him, his weight pressing me against the floor.

His hands framed my face, then slid down to my shoulders, my waist, leaving trails of scorching heat through my clothes. I arched against him, my own hands exploring the broad expanse of his shoulders, the strong column of his neck, the silk of his hair.

"Leila," he breathed against my lips, then trailed kisses along my jaw, down to the sensitive spot where my neck met my shoulder. I gasped, and my fingers tightened in his hair.

"I've wanted this for so long," I whispered. The confession tore from me. Even though I knew it might break the spell we were under, I had to say it.

His eyes were black with desire as he leaned away to look into mine. "You have no idea," he said roughly. "Watching you, wanting you, telling myself all the reasons I couldn't have you."

"Stop telling yourself anything," I said, arching up to kiss him again. "Stop thinking so much."

His hand slid under my jumper, and he rested his palm flat against my stomach. The skin-to-skin contact was electric and overwhelming.

"Please," I whispered, though I wasn't sure what I was begging for. Everything. Anything. Him.

His hand moved higher, and his fingers traced the edge of my bra. When his palm covered my breast, we both groaned. Even through the thin fabric, the sensation was overwhelming.

"You're so perfect," he murmured against my throat. "So bloody perfect."

He pushed my jumper up, and I helped him pull it over my head. There was only heat now, only him, only this moment we'd been racing toward since the day we met.

His eyes traveled over me with reverence that made my chest tight. "Beautiful," he breathed, then lowered his head, pressing kisses to the swell of my breast.

The sight of him—all that controlled power, the defined muscles of his chest and arms—made my mouth go dry.

I ran my hands over his pecs, feeling the heat of his skin, the racing of his heart.

We were skin to skin now, and the sensation was almost too much. I was drowning in him, in his scent, his touch, the weight of him. I gasped into his mouth when his hand found my breast again and his thumb brushed over my hardened nipple.

"I need—" I said, but I couldn't find words for the ache building inside me.

"I know," he said roughly. "I know, love."

He reached behind me, unclasping my bra with one hand, and then his mouth was on me, taking my nipple between his lips. I cried out as waves of sensation crashed through me.

The world narrowed to this—his mouth on me, his hands holding me steady.

The storm raging outside was nothing compared to the one building between us.

6

Tag

Every wall I'd built crumbled as I got lost in Leila's mouth, hot and demanding against mine. I buried my hands in her silky hair, angling her head to deepen the kiss, and swallowed the soft sounds she made. She tasted like whiskey mixed with desire, want, and need—the things I'd denied myself for far too long.

The fire roared beside us, casting wild shadows on the walls, but its heat was nothing compared to what burned between us. Every reason I'd kept her at arm's length, every time I'd called her "kid" to maintain separation, all fell away under the weight of her response.

She arched against me, seeking more, and I gave it to her. My mouth traveled from her lips to her jaw, down to that spot where her neck met her shoulder that had tormented me for so long. She gasped when my teeth grazed the sensitive skin there, and her fingers tightened in my hair enough to hurt.

"Tag." She murmured my name like a prayer. Christ, the way she said it nearly destroyed what little control I had left.

I groaned against her throat when her nails dragged across my back. Every touch was like redemption and damnation rolled into one. The storm we'd endured thus far was nothing compared to the hunger and passion that tangled into something I couldn't fight anymore.

I pulled away, both of us breathing hard. Her lips were swollen from my kisses, and her chest rose and fell as she fought for air. We stared at each other, the weight of what we were about to do settling over us.

I was at a crossroads. I had time to remind myself of the promise I'd made Idris and of my vow never to marry.

"Leila…" Each time I repeated her name, my voice came out rough and broken, betraying everything I felt.

She must have heard the hesitation, because her hands framed my face and her thumbs brushed against the stubble on my jaw. "Don't," she whispered with fierce determination. "Don't you dare pull away now. Not after all this time. Not after this torture."

All this time. She was right. Three years of my body burning every time she entered a room, watching other men notice and approach her while I stood in the shadows, grinding my teeth to dust.

Every instinct that had kept me alive through countless missions screamed at me to stop.

But I couldn't.

I studied her face one more time. She was the most beautiful thing I'd ever seen, and at this moment, she was mine. Even if only for these stolen days.

I stood, lifting her with me. She wrapped her legs around my waist without hesitation, and I carried her to the bed.

She gasped at the movement, then her mouth found my neck, lips and tongue and teeth working against my pulse point. The sensation of her weight in my arms, solid and real and warm, threatened to bring me to my knees.

"You're going to kill me," I muttered against her hair on our way to the bed. My hands gripped her arse, holding her steady.

The bed frame creaked ominously under our combined weight as I lowered her onto the heavy blankets.

I followed her down, unable to break contact, needing her beneath me. But as I braced myself above her, gazing down at her face illuminated by firelight, sanity made one last desperate attempt.

"If we do this…" Each word fought its way out. "When we leave here, when the storm passes and the roads clear—this ends."

Understanding dawned in her eyes, and pain flickered across her features before she controlled it, and the glimpse of hurt nearly broke my resolve. But I had to be clear. I had to protect us both from false hope.

"I can't promise you more than the days we're here," I continued, hating myself more with each syllable. "I can't give you forever. I won't give you marriage or a white picket fence or whatever normal people have. My parents—"

"I know," she interrupted, her voice steady despite the tears gathering in her eyes. "And I understand that you're scared." Her hands moved to my shoulders, not pushing me away, but not pulling me closer either. "And you need to know that I'm not asking for forever." Her voice softened. "I'm not asking you to change your mind or make promises you can't keep. I'm asking for now. Can you give me that?"

The rational part of my brain screamed countless warnings. This would only make leaving harder. This would only cause us both more pain when it ended. This was a mistake of epic proportions.

But looking down at her, seeing the acceptance in her eyes along with the want, I realized I'd already lost this battle. I'd lost it the moment we set foot in this castle. Hell, maybe I'd lost it years before when I realized that, despite every attempt not to, she was the woman I fantasized about endlessly.

"This won't end well," I warned, one last attempt at sanity.

"I know."

"You'll hate me when it's over."

"No," she said with complete certainty. "I could never hate you, Tag. Even if you break my heart, even if this destroys me, I could never hate you."

"Leila—" I began again.

"Tag, please," she said, tracing a scar on my ribs from a knife wound in Prague, then another on my shoulder from a bullet graze in Beirut. "So many," she murmured, her touch featherlight.

"Occupational hazard." My voice came out rougher than intended as her fingers continued their exploration.

I reached for the waistband of her leggings, hooking my thumbs in the elastic. "Lift up," I said softly, and when she did, I peeled them down her legs, taking my time, revealing strong thighs, the curve of her calves, and the delicate bones of her ankles. The black knickers she wore matched her bra. Neither left much to the imagination.

"Christ." I sat on my heels, looking at her. "You're—"

"Your turn," she said again, emboldened now, reaching for the drawstring of my track pants.

I helped her push them down, along with my boxers, until we were both nearly naked. The firelight played across her skin, highlighting curves and shadows. I had to close my eyes for a moment against the rush of want that threatened to overwhelm me.

"Look at me," she whispered.

My breath caught when I opened my lids and witnessed her open desire. I hooked my fingers in her knickers and drew them down slowly.

"Beautiful," I breathed, meaning it with every fiber of my being. She explored the terrain of my chest with a reverence that made my breath catch—tracing scars from old missions, mapping the muscles with her fingertips like she was trying to memorize me.

I let my gaze linger on her nakedness, keeping her as warm as I could with the scorching heat that flowed through my body.

"You're staring," she said, a hint of vulnerability creeping into her voice.

"You're incredible," I replied, meaning it.

I lowered my mouth to her neck, tasting the salt on her skin. Her hands tangled in my hair as I moved lower.

"Tag, please," she gasped, arching beneath me.

Her dark nipples were already hard with arousal when I lowered my head to take one into my mouth.

She cried out, arching off the bed, her nails digging into my flesh hard enough to leave marks. Good. I wanted evidence that this had been real, that I hadn't dreamed it.

I lavished attention on one breast, then the other, drunk on the sounds she made and the way she writhed beneath me. The sensation of her nakedness against my own nearly ended things before they'd properly begun. She was so soft, so warm, so completely fitted against me.

"I need you," she whispered against my mouth. "God, Tag, I've needed you for so long."

Her words left me breathless. I kissed her again, deep and desperate, pouring suppressed want into it as I reached between her legs and her wetness coated my fingers.

I took my time exploring her sex, learning what made her gasp and what made her moan. When I thrust two fingers inside, she was so wet and ready. The knowledge that I'd done this to her, that she wanted me this much, had me on the edge of climaxing again far too soon.

I stroked her, watching her expression as it changed. She was so responsive, so open in her pleasure. There were no masks, no walls, just Leila coming apart under my touch.

"Tag, please," she gasped. "I need all of you. Now."

"Are you sure?" I asked, positioning myself at her entrance and forcing myself to go slow despite every instinct screaming at me to claim her.

"I've never been more sure of anything," she said, wrapping her legs around me. "Please, Tag. I need this. I need you."

When I pushed forward, discovering how tight she was, everything stopped.

The resistance was unmistakable, undeniable. My entire body went rigid as the reality of it crashed through me.

"Leila?"

I saw the flush on her cheeks, the way she bit her lip, and the guilty look that confirmed what I'd just realized.

"You're a virgin." Not a question. A statement. A revelation that changed everything.

She nodded, not meeting my eyes.

"Why didn't you tell me?" The words came out harsher than intended, but Christ, what had she been thinking?

"Because you would have stopped," she whispered. Her eyes were bright with unshed tears. "You would have done the noble thing and stopped, and I couldn't bear it. Not after waiting so long."

"Of course I would have stopped. Your first time shouldn't be—" I struggled for words, but my brain short-circuited. "It shouldn't be with someone who can't offer you a future. You should have someone who can promise you tomorrow and mean it."

"There's never been anyone else," she said. "Only you. It's only ever been you, Tag."

My God, she'd been waiting. For me. Only me.

"I didn't save myself for marriage or for some perfect moment in a rose petal-covered bed. I saved myself for the only man I've ever wanted."

Her confession staggered me. This would be her first time. Her first everything. A memory she'd carry for the rest of her life, and I was the one who would give it to her. Not someone who could promise her forever. Not someone who could give her the future she deserved. Me. A man so damaged by his parents' toxic marriage that he'd sworn off love entirely.

I should stop. Every shred of honor I possessed demanded I stop, that I protect her from this mistake, from the inevitable heartbreak.

But I searched her face for doubt, for hesitation, for anything that would give me the strength to be the better man and end this. All I saw was certainty. Want. Trust. Even love, as much as I wanted to deny it.

And I was too selfish, too weak, too desperate for her to do the right thing.

"This will hurt," I warned, my voice breaking on the words.

"I know and I trust you." She pulled me down for a kiss, soft this time, almost tender.

I kissed her deeply, trying to tell her without words everything I couldn't say aloud. Then I moved forward again, as slowly as I could manage, watching for any sign of pain. I saw the moment it hit—her breath caught, her body tensed, and her fingers dug into my biceps.

"Breathe, love," I whispered against her lips. "I've got you."

I held absolutely motionless though, every muscle in my body screaming at me to move. She was so tight around me, so warm, and it took every ounce of control not to thrust deeper.

Her body relaxed gradually, adjusting. Every instinct screamed at me to claim, to take, but this wasn't about me. This was about her, about making this good for her, about giving her something worth the wait, even if I couldn't give her forever.

"Okay?" I managed to ask when her eyes met mine.

"More than okay. Is it always—does it always feel like this?" The wonder I heard in her voice made me want to roar.

"No," I admitted. "It's never been like this."

And it hadn't. During all my controlled encounters, brief liaisons that never lasted past dawn, it had never felt like…coming home. Like completion. Like finding something I hadn't known I was missing.

She was silk and fire wrapped around me, her body slowly accepting mine. The sensation was overwhelming—not just physical, though that alone threatened to undo me—but the emotional weight of it. This meant something. This changed everything, even if I couldn't let it.

She moved against me experimentally, and I nearly lost all control. "Please, Tag. I need—"

I started slow, pulling out slightly before pressing forward again. Each movement was deliberate as I fought every instinct that demanded I take her harder and faster.

"Tell me if it's too much," I said against her mouth.

"It's not enough," she gasped, her hips lifting to meet mine. "More, Tag. Please."

I shifted the angle, and she cried out.

"There," she moaned. "Right there."

Soon, she moved with me as her initial tension was replaced by growing pleasure. Her soft gasps turned to moans that I swallowed with kisses. The heat between us built, our bodies slick with sweat despite the cold air. The fire crackled beside us, but I barely heard it over the sound of her breathing, the small sounds she made, and the way she said my name like a prayer.

I reached between us, finding her sensitive bundle of nerves, and circled it with my thumb. She keened and arched off the bed.

"That's it," I encouraged. "Let go, love."

"Tag," she said my name over and over. "Oh God, Tag—"

When she came apart beneath me, my name on her lips, her body clenching around me, pulsing and tight and perfect, I followed her over the edge, pulling out before I came, at the last possible second, finishing on her stomach with a groan that came from somewhere deep in my chest, wishing so hard that I could stay buried in the woman I'd tried so hard not to love.

For several seconds, neither of us moved. I was braced above her, both of us breathing hard as the reality of what we'd done settled over us like a blanket.

"Stay here," I said softly, pressing a kiss to her forehead before pulling away. Guilt twisted in my gut when she winced, and I grabbed my discarded shirt to gently clean her stomach, then her thighs, noting the small amount of blood with a fresh wave of protective fury.

"Are you hurt?" I asked, my voice rougher than intended.

"No," she said, reaching for me.

"Let me—" I began, but she pulled me down beside her.

"I'm fine, Tag. Better than fine." She smiled, and it transformed her face. "That was…"

"Yeah," I agreed, because there were no words adequate for what we'd experienced together.

Sweat cooled on our skin as we both fought to catch our breath. I pulled more of the heavy blankets over us, cocooning us in our own world.

She curled into my side, and her head found the spot on my chest that seemed made for her. Her fingers traced lazy patterns through the hair there.

Neither of us spoke for several minutes.

"No regrets," she finally said, so quiet I almost missed it. "This is my choice. My memory to keep. Whatever happens when we leave here, I'll have this."

I understood what she was doing—protecting herself already, building walls against the inevitable pain, preparing for the end before we'd even had a middle. My arms tightened around her involuntarily, as if I could keep her through sheer force of will.

"Leila—"

"Don't," she interrupted. "Don't make promises you can't keep. Don't tell me pretty lies to make me feel better. Let me have this. It's enough."

But it wasn't. Not even close.

Neither of us spoke of love. But it was there in the way she curled into me like she belonged there, in the way I held her like she might disappear if I loosened my grip.

The truth settled into my bones with absolute certainty. I was deeply, irrevocably taken with Leila Nassar.

The realization terrified me—this was exactly what I'd sworn never to let happen. But I couldn't move, couldn't let go, couldn't do anything but hold her and accept this truth even if it changed nothing.

Leila raised her head. "Whatever you're thinking or planning, whatever noble sacrifice you're contemplating—don't."

I nodded and pressed a kiss to her forehead.

She settled against my chest, and I held her, the woman I couldn't resist, and tried not to think about how empty my arms would be when she was gone.

7

Nightingale

Tag's arms tightened around me as I shifted against him, and he kissed my temple.

"Are you all right?" His voice was rough with concern. "Did I hurt you?"

"No," I said, though when I moved again, I couldn't hide my wince. The truth was, my body ached in unfamiliar ways—a deep soreness between my legs, tender places where his mouth had been, muscles I'd never used before protesting new activity.

"Leila." He shifted so he could see my face. "I should have been gentler. I should have—"

"You were perfect." I touched his cheek. "It was perfect."

His hand moved to my hip, not with desire this time but with care. "Give me a few minutes, then I'll come get you."

I sat up when he got out of bed. "Wait. Where are you going?"

"I'm going to run you a bath."

I was about to protest, given how cold it was, then realized that sometime in the last hour, the heat must've kicked on. When he turned on the light, I knew the generator had too.

"Stay where you are, Nightingale."

My heart lurched at his use of the code name I'd received from him, and while I waited for his return, I thought about that night. It was the third week of training for the unit, and the focus was on communications when there were multiple assets to manage, each requiring a different accent, and sometimes a different persona.

I'd switched between a Russian arms dealer's mistress, a frightened British tourist, an elderly Syrian grandmother, and a young French student, pushing myself to prove to him specifically that I'd not only get through the training, but I'd excel at it.

Afterwards, Tag had pulled me aside. "You sing in any voice needed," he'd said, his expression as unreadable as ever. "Like a nightingale. In fact, that's your code name."

"Yeah?" I'd asked, trying to sound casual despite the way my pulse quickened at his approval.

"It suits you," was all he'd said before turning away, leaving me with a memory more intimate than he'd probably intended. Or maybe that was my imagination, the same that had been reading too much into every word he said since we'd met.

"Come on," he said, stepping out of the bathroom and over to the bed. "Time for me to take care of you." Before I could stand, Tag lifted me in his arms as if I weighed nothing. I buried my face in his neck as he carried me to the oversized claw-foot tub and gently set me in it before climbing in behind me.

I sighed as the warm water enveloped me, easing the ache between my legs and soothing my muscles.

"Let me," he said when I reached for the washcloth and soap.

His touch was infinitely gentle as he moved over my skin with reverent care. He washed my hair, massaging my scalp until I was nearly purring. When he helped me lean back to rinse, his hand supported me.

"Better?" he asked.

"Much." I caught his hand, bringing it to my lips. "Thank you."

"I'm not finished yet," he said with a sly grin as he reached between my legs, parting my folds with soapy fingers. "Does this hurt?" he whispered.

I quivered when his thumb pressed against my clit. "Not at all," I managed to say even as my brain struggled with remembering what words were.

"Come for me, Leila," he murmured as his fingers worked their magic.

As if responding to his command, my body clenched, and pleasure like I'd never known until tonight seized every muscle.

"Breathe, love," he said, trailing kisses down my neck, making me shudder all the more.

We sat in the warm water for a few more minutes, but when it cooled off, he shifted me forward.

"Stay here," he said.

Tag returned with one of his shirts and a towel he'd warmed by the fire. He helped me from the bath and dried me off, patting me dry as if I were made of glass. The shirt was soft from wear and smelled like him.

"Sleepy?" he asked when I tried to hide my yawn.

"Aren't you?"

He smirked. "Honestly?"

"Always."

"I can't imagine closing my eyes with you beside me, wearing nothing but my shirt."

We crawled under the blankets, and soon, the shirt was on the floor and our naked bodies were once again pressed together.

"Teach me," I said, shy as I reached for him.

He took my hand and wrapped it around his length. "You won't break me, love," he said, tightening my grip as he showed me how to move up and down. When he shuddered like I had in the bath and closed his eyes, I was more empowered than I had been when I was invited to officially join Unit 23.

"What did I do wrong?" I asked when he covered my hand, then removed it.

"Nothing, love, but when I come again, I want to be inside you." He reached for a packet on the nightstand and opened it with his teeth.

"Can I help?" I asked.

He held out his palm, and I picked up the condom. "Put it on the tip, then roll it down," he said, resting his arms at his sides.

"What if I don't do it right?"

His eyes had drifted closed, but he opened one. "You're doing it right, Leila. So right."

When he smiled, I did too, and when he rolled me over, spread my legs with his knee, then pressed against me, I strained, trying to get nearer.

"So anxious," he said, moving through my wetness.

"My God, that feels amazing," I said, arching my back more as a reflex than anything intentional.

"You are amazing, sweet Leila." His jaw tightened, and I watched, wanting to see—to remember—how he looked when he came.

After making love again the next morning, we lay in bed, both quiet after experiencing another mind-blowing climax.

"Hungry?" Tag asked.

"Ravenous."

We made our way to the kitchen, where he insisted I sit while he prepared food. He moved around the space like he'd lived here all his life, scrambling eggs, toasting bread, and brewing tea.

"I used to imagine this," I admitted. "You cooking for me. Us being domestic together."

He glanced over his shoulder. "Yeah? What else did you imagine?"

Heat crept up my neck. "Things."

"What kind of things?" He set a plate in front of me, then took the chair across from me. "Tell me."

"Tag…"

"I want to know." His foot found mine under the table. "I want to know everything you thought about. Everything you wanted."

I took a bite of eggs to buy time, but he wouldn't relent.

"I used to imagine you coming to Damascus and not leaving. Staying in my apartment. Waking up with you."

"What else?"

"You touching me." The words came out barely above a whisper. "I was in love with you," I said quietly. "Even then."

He froze. "Leila—"

"I know." I forced a smile. "I don't expect you to say it too. I know this is…whatever this is. But I wanted you to know."

He stood abruptly, coming around the table to pull me to my feet. His hands framed my face, and when he kissed me, it was with a tenderness that made my chest ache. "Let's go upstairs," he said against my lips. "Let me show you…let me…" He struggled for words, then gave up, kissing me again instead.

This time when we made love, he treated me like I was precious. He laid me out on the bed, worshiping every inch of my skin with his mouth, avoiding the places that were too sore. When I tried to reciprocate, he caught my hands.

"This is for you," he said. "Let me give you this."

He used his mouth and fingers to bring me to the edge over and over, easing off each time until I was begging, my mind blank from the intensity of it. When he finally let me come, it was with his mouth on me, his fingers gentle inside me, and I shattered so completely I thought I might never find all the pieces again.

Afterwards, he held me, whispering soft words against my hair. "So beautiful. So perfect. Mine."

"Yours," I agreed, and he shuddered against me.

We dozed for a while, wrapped around each other. When I woke, gray light was filtering through the windows. The rain was still falling, but lighter now, less violent. The storm was breaking.

Tag was awake, his fingers tracing lazy patterns on my bare shoulder.

"Morning," he murmured.

"Is it?"

"I've no idea, to be honest. How are you?"

I took inventory. Sore in places, but not unbearably so.

"Good," I said. "Really good."

"Liar." But he was smiling. "Stay here. I'll run you another bath."

"Stay with me instead."

He didn't need more invitation than that. We made love again, slow and tender as he watched for any sign of discomfort. There was some—I was too new at this for there not to be—but the pleasure far outweighed the pain.

"I could get used to this," I said afterwards, sprawled across his chest, listening to his heartbeat.

His arms tightened around me, but he didn't respond, and that should have been my first warning. Instead, I was too lost in the afterglow, too drunk on the sensation of finally having what I'd wanted for so long, to fret over the way he'd tensed at my words.

We stayed in bed a couple more hours, talking and touching. He told me about his childhood at

Glenshadow, about the cattle he raised, about his sister, who lived in Edinburgh, and his brother, who worked in Glasgow. I told him about growing up as a diplomat's daughter, about learning languages by necessity, about how lost I'd been after Idris died until Unit 23 gave me purpose again.

"I was terrified that first day," I admitted. "When you and Typhon came to the funeral, it was as though you were cataloging my weaknesses."

"We were," he admitted. "As you know, it's what we do. Assess threats, capabilities, weaknesses."

"I was so afraid I'd fail."

"You didn't. In fact, you were magnificent." He pressed a kiss to my forehead. "You still are."

It was midafternoon when hunger finally drove us to the kitchen. Tag insisted on making a late lunch while I showered. The hot water stung in places that made me blush, remembering how they'd gotten so sensitive. When I emerged, dressed in one of his shirts and a pair of leggings I'd found in my bag, the heat in his eyes had desire pooling between my legs again.

We were halfway through the meal when a knock came at the door.

"Who is it?" I asked when he stood to look.

"The MacLeods," he responded, inviting them inside.

"The storm is breaking," Mr. MacLeod announced as he set another food-laden basket on the counter. "Should clear by tomorrow, maybe the day after. Roads will be passable soon enough."

Tomorrow. The word lodged in my throat. I'd been so lost in the bubble of last night and this morning that I'd forgotten about the world outside.

"That's…good news," Tag said, though the tone of his voice suggested otherwise.

After they left a few minutes later, I stood at the window as rain fell. It was definitely lighter outside, the sky less oppressively dark. As Mr. MacLeod had said, we'd be able to leave tomorrow or the next day. And then what?

"Hey." Tag's arms came around me from behind. "You're frowning. Why?"

"I'm wondering what happens when we leave here."

"We don't have to think about that yet." He pressed a kiss to my neck. "We still have time."

"And then?"

He was quiet long enough for me to wonder if he'd answer. "Then we return to work. Resume finding out who was following you and why."

"Right," I said. "Of course."

He turned me to face him. "Leila—"

"It's fine." I managed a smile. "I understand. You made it clear that this would only last as long as we were here."

"That's not what I—" He stopped, frustrated. "It's complicated."

"It really isn't." I pulled away from him. "We should check the rest of the castle. Make sure the storm hasn't done any damage."

It appeared as though there was something more he wanted to say, but after waiting a few minutes, I went upstairs to put on warmer clothes.

We spent the afternoon wandering through the tunnels again, though things between us seemed so different. Tag was affectionate and tender, but I'd withdrawn, building the walls I'd need once we left Dunravin. He noticed—I could see it in the way he studied me, the way he'd reach for me then stop himself—but neither of us addressed it directly.

As evening fell, he suggested we dine together. "Mrs. MacLeod brought dinner," he said. "And there's wine. We could—"

"I'm not hungry. In fact, I need some air." I stalked out the door, hoping he would follow as much as I hoped he wouldn't.

I paced the castle grounds as the sun set, breathing in the rain-washed air. The landscape showed evidence of the storm's violence—branches down, debris scattered—but Dunravin stood unmarked. It had weathered centuries of storms and would for several more, even in its somewhat dilapidated state.

When I returned, the kitchen had been transformed, with candles, the table set with the castle's best china, and wine breathing in a crystal decanter I hadn't known existed.

"What's all this?" I asked, wishing I hadn't sounded so unappreciative.

"You deserve romance, Leila." He pulled out my chair. "You deserve so much more than I can give you."

The honesty of it stole my breath. "Tag—"

"Let's not talk about it." He poured wine, hands not quite steady. "Let's enjoy tonight."

So we did. We ate and drank and conversed about things that were safe—books, music, places we'd traveled. He told me funny stories about Con, Ash, and Gus from their childhood. I told him about the time I'd accidentally insulted a Syrian general's mother while trying to compliment her cooking. We laughed and let the wine warm us and didn't talk about tomorrow.

Later, in bed, our lovemaking had an edge of desperation. We came together again and again through the night, as if we could stop time through sheer will. I memorized how he felt inside me, the weight of him above me, the way he said my name when he came. He mapped every inch of my body with his hands and mouth, finding places that made me cry out, teaching me pleasures I hadn't known existed.

"Stay with me," he whispered at one point, though I was right there beneath him.

But I knew he didn't mean forever.

When he finally slept, exhausted, I lay awake, listening to the rain. It was barely a drizzle now. Tomorrow, the sun would shine. The helicopter would come. We'd leave this place and go back to being who we were before—two people held apart by duty and fear.

I turned to study his face in the dim light. Asleep, he looked younger, the lines of tension smoothed away. I wanted to kiss him awake, to beg him to choose me, choose us, choose something more than these stolen days.

Instead, I closed my eyes, knowing I'd need this memory to keep me warm through all the cold, lonely nights ahead.

My mobile's shrill ring shattered the morning peace. Tag stirred beside me but didn't wake as I extracted myself from his embrace and padded to where the device was charging.

"Nightingale," I answered quietly, moving into the bathroom and closing the door.

"Good to hear your voice." Viper's tone was clipped but relieved. "Typhon briefed me on the extraction to Dunravin. Are you holding up all right?"

"Yes, ma'am. The safe house was definitely compromised—"

"We know, and you cannot return to London at this time. Typhon and I agree you should lie low somewhere else until we can narrow down who was surveilling you."

"Understood. When's the extraction scheduled?"

"Tomorrow morning, weather permitting."

"Yes, ma'am."

"And, Nightingale? Good instincts getting out when you did."

I ended the call and stood in the bathroom, processing. When I emerged, Tag was awake, sitting on the edge of the bed, his own mobile beside him.

"Viper?" he asked.

I nodded. "You?"

"Typhon." He stood, moving toward me. "We're not returning to London."

"I know. Viper said she and Typhon would coordinate a new location prior to extraction."

"We have done."

My stomach clenched. *We?* "So, where?"

"Glenshadow. I suggested it, Typhon agreed. It's isolated, defensible, and off anyone's radar."

His *home*. I couldn't stay in his house, surrounded by his things, playing the role of just another operative under his protection while my heart broke a little more each day.

"I have other options," I countered.

"No. You don't. Not until we know who was after you in London."

I didn't care for his tone. "Why are you acting like this decision is yours to make?"

His head cocked, and he glared at me the same way I was at him. "I suppose because I made the decision about Dunravin."

"You did? Not Typhon?"

"We decided together in the same way we did Glenshadow."

"No," I said, turning to leave the room. He caught up with me before I reached the stairs.

"No? Leila, wait. You're being—"

I spun around on him. "*You* don't make decisions on my behalf. Not anymore."

His hand touched my shoulder. "Talk to me. What's really going on here? Is this reaction because we agreed that our affair would end when we left Dunravin?"

"How dare you?" I seethed, jerking away from him.

"I *dare* because I don't understand your behavior."

Every muscle in my body went rigid in anger. My behavior? "I knew this was temporary as well as you did. It was the only reason I agreed to it in the first place."

His eyes bored into mine in a way that said he knew I was lying. Which I was. But that was beside the point. What I needed to figure out—on my own—was what my next step should be. Should I agree to go to Glenshadow for the time being while I planned my own *extraction*? That would make the most sense. It would give me the opportunity to reach out to my assets and craft a plan to disappear. It wouldn't be the first time, even recently. It had taken Tag weeks to find me. This time, I intended for it to take months. Long enough for my shattered heart to mend. Long enough to move on from my obsession with Niall MacTaggert. To get over him.

"I know what you're doing," he said, leaning against the wall and folding his arms.

"And what is that?"

The bastard smirked. "You're running, and I won't allow it."

8

Tag

The words left my mouth before I could stop them. We stood in the bedroom at Dunravin, morning light filtering through windows streaked with rain from the storm. It was zero seven hundred hours. The extraction wasn't until tomorrow morning—we had another full day here, but I was already losing her.

Rather than argue, she simply looked at me with those eyes that gave away nothing, then turned and walked out of the room.

I followed her downstairs, my bare feet silent on the cold stone. She stood facing the window, still wearing my shirt from last night.

"We don't need to do this again," she said without turning around. "You've made your position clear. When we leave Dunravin, this ends. I accepted that."

"Then, why are you planning to disappear?"

She turned then, one eyebrow raised. "What makes you think I'm planning anything?"

"I know you, Leila. I can see it—the way you're already building walls, creating distance."

"I'm being professional. Isn't that what you wanted?"

"You can't just vanish. Not when—"

"When what?" She cut me off. "When I was the one who spotted the surveillance? When I aborted the extraction to save both myself and the agent they were sending? I've kept myself alive for three years, Tag. I don't need you to—"

"To what? Care about you? Want you safe?"

"To make decisions for me." She turned back to the window. "You and Typhon deciding I should go to Glenshadow. You deciding what's best. Always you deciding."

"I'm terrified of losing you." The admission came out rough and desperate.

She turned slowly. "And yet, we have no future, isn't that right? How can you lose me if you don't have me in the first place?"

I gripped my hair, pulling it. "I don't know how to do this," I said. "I don't know how to—"

"There's nothing left to say, Tag. We made an agreement, and now, we have to stick to it." She turned to leave. "You made your feelings abundantly clear, and the last thing I want is to hear them again."

I moved faster, getting between her and the doorway, backing her against the wall. "I can't let you go," I said, pressing my body flush with hers so she could feel exactly how much I wanted her. Needed her.

"You have to—"

"Tell me you don't want this. Tell me you don't want me."

Her eyes bored into mine. "It doesn't matter what I want. It's never mattered what I want."

Our mouths were an inch apart, and the air between us was charged with anger and desire. I don't know who moved first—maybe we both did—but suddenly, we were kissing. This wasn't tender like our first time, or desperate like last night. This was angry and raw, full of frustration and want and denial exploding between us.

"I hate you," she gasped against my mouth, her hands fisting in my hair like my own had.

"I know."

"I hate that you're doing this to us."

"I know."

"I hate that I can't stop wanting you."

Her legs wrapped around my waist when I lifted her, and we stumbled toward the carpet in front of the cold fireplace. We tore at each other's clothes until we were both naked, then pressed our bodies as close as we could get. Leila's nails raked down my back hard enough to draw blood, and my teeth marked her shoulder. It was an exorcism of everything we couldn't say, couldn't be, couldn't have.

She cried out when I entered her, not from pain but from the overwhelming intensity of it. We met, thrust for thrust, pounding into each other while our mouths and tongues battled in their own way.

"God, Leila, I—"

She raised her hand and covered my mouth. "Don't." She rolled us to our sides with strength I wasn't ready for, but instead of leaving, she pushed me onto my back and straddled me. "*I'm* in control, Tag. Me."

I nodded, staring into her beautiful eyes, wishing I could tell her how much I loved her, even if it changed nothing. Instead, I brought my hands to her breasts, tugging at her nipples until her back arched and I could feel her body begin to clench mine.

I rolled us like she'd done to me, driving my cock as deep and as hard as I could into her pussy. She grabbed for my arms as if holding onto me to keep herself from spiraling into the pleasure she was trying so hard not to allow. I thrust more, leaned down, and took a nipple into my mouth, sucking hard, then biting before soothing it with my tongue. When I did it again, Leila came apart in my arms, thrashing as much as writhing, screaming my name again and again. I stayed with her as long as I could, but as soon as I knew I couldn't hold back any longer, I pulled out, releasing on her stomach.

Leila turned her head, but I could still see her tears, hating that I was the one who caused them to fall.

Grabbing my shirt, I wiped her stomach. She pulled away without looking at me, gathering her scattered clothes. "This changes nothing," she said as she left the room without putting them on.

"I know."

I stayed on the library floor, staring at the ceiling with its ancient beams, wondering how something that felt so right could be so wrong.

I returned to the bedroom, showered off the evidence of what we'd done, then lay on the bed fully dressed. Waiting. One hour turned into five. I could hear her downstairs but couldn't bring myself to seek her out any more than she'd come to me.

Eventually, I drifted to sleep, wrung out from sex and anger and pain. When I woke again, I could hear her in the hallway outside the bedroom door. I sat up, threw my legs over the side of the bed, and went to her.

Her eyes were swollen and bloodshot from crying, and her shoulders rolled forward as if she was trying to make herself smaller, invisible. "Leila…"

"I need my things."

I reached for her. "Come to bed."

She jerked away from me. "I just need my things. I'll sleep in the other room."

"Please don't do this," I begged.

"This is on you, Tag. Not me."

I nodded once. She was right, and I was powerless to change it.

I lay awake the rest of the night, talking myself into going to her, lying beside her, just holding her. Then, I'd talk myself out of it.

Zero two hundred came and went. Then three. Then finally, at four, I heard it—the quiet sound of her door opening, the soft footsteps of someone trying not to be heard. I listened as her heavy boots landed on each step of the staircase, then counted several seconds before slipping out of the room. I raced down the servants' stairs, the ones that would get me to the main entrance before her.

When she turned the corner, pack over her shoulder, I was leaning against the door, waiting.

"Going somewhere?" I asked.

She froze, resignation replacing surprise on her face. "Let me go," she whispered.

"You know I can't." I straightened.

"Why not?" Her voice broke, and she turned her back to me.

"If anything happened to you, it would destroy me."

She faced me again, wiping at her tears. "Then we'd be even."

She fought as I pulled her into my arms, but soon, she buried her head in my chest and sobbed.

Eventually, I carried her up the main staircase and rested her body on the bed we'd shared. I covered her with blankets, then lay behind her with our bodies flush.

"Don't make me go to Glenshadow," she whispered.

"You'll be safe there."

She shook her head. "I won't."

"I promise you will be."

"The only way you can keep that promise is if you aren't there too."

Understanding dawned on me. What Leila was saying was that, more than whoever followed her to London, I represented the most danger.

Within minutes, she was sound asleep.

When she woke with the sun, we were in the same position.

"What time do we leave?" she asked without raising her head.

"Eleven hundred."

"You're a bastard," she whispered.

"Yes," I agreed.

"Just because I'm going with you, doesn't mean you win."

"I'm not trying to win. I'm trying to keep you alive."

We lay side by side for another few hours until I heard someone knock on the kitchen door.

"That's probably the MacLeods," I said. "I'll go let them in."

Leila's eyes were on me, and I knew she'd heard what I said, but when she didn't respond, I left the room and rushed downstairs.

"*Madainn mhath,*" Mrs. MacLeod said with a wink.

"Good morning to you as well."

"I've come with food for your journey."

I nodded once. "So you've heard we're leaving today."

"Aye. The wee Cavendish rang."

I chuckled at her reference to Renegade. I doubted anyone else in Scotland would refer to him as "wee." I was six feet five, and he had at least two inches on me.

"How does it look out there?" I asked when Mr. MacLeod joined us inside a few minutes later.

"The landing pad is clear," he responded. "The storm did some damage, but nothing that will interfere with the helicopter being able to land."

"Thank you," I said.

He smiled. "It's what we're here for."

"Take care of the lass," his wife said, patting my arm.

"I will do. I promise."

"Come now, Grunny. We've got work to get to." Mr. MacLeod held out his arm, and she took it.

"We'll look forward to your next visit, Mr. MacTaggert."

The helicopter arrived exactly at eleven hundred hours, cutting through the Highland mist that still clung to the mountains. I recognized the aircraft as belonging to Con, and the man flying it was Callum, who served as his pilot, chauffeur, and bodyguard. He also had MI6-level security clearance.

Leila had come downstairs a few minutes ago, packed and ready to leave, but looking much the same way she had the day of her brother's funeral.

We loaded our gear in silence, climbed in, and buckled up. Seconds later, we lifted off, leaving Dunravin behind.

The Scottish Highlands spread beneath us—muted purple heather, silver lochs reflecting the gray sky, and mountains wrapped in clouds. Leila stared out the window, deliberately not looking at me, her reflection showing the exhaustion and hurt she was trying to hide.

An hour later, Glenshadow came into view—my family seat rising from the landscape like something from another era. The stone walls and arched windows of the fifteenth-century monastery my ancestors had claimed and converted had remained mostly unchanged since medieval times. On the other hand, the interior had been updated on numerous occasions. The estate spread around it, thousands of acres where I raised cattle and tried to forget that my real work involved killing people for the Crown.

"It's beautiful," Leila said quietly, surprising me.

"It's been in my family for three hundred years. The monastery itself is older."

"A sanctuary turned fortress."

"Something like that."

I watched as she took in everything as we descended—approaches, exits, defensive positions, potential infiltration points. Even exhausted, she was professional. Always thinking, analyzing, preparing.

When we touched down on the east lawn, Mrs. Murray, my housekeeper, stood at the main entrance despite not knowing exactly when we'd arrive. The woman had an uncanny ability to sense when I was coming home, even unscheduled. She'd been with my family for forty years and had practically raised me after my mother left.

"Mr. MacTaggert, welcome home," she muttered in an accent thick with disapproval as she took in our disheveled state.

"Apologies for the lack of notice, Mrs. Murray. This is Miss Nassar. She'll be staying with us. Could you prepare the Blue Room for an extended stay?"

From the corner of my eye, I saw Leila raise a brow.

"Of course." Mrs. Murray greeted her with surprising warmth. "You'll be wanting something to eat after your journey, miss. I'll have food sent up while you settle in."

"That's very kind of you," Leila said, earning another smile from my housekeeper.

"We'll be using my study as an operations center," I said when I saw Douglas, my estate manager and head of security, approach. "We'll need the historical archives brought up from the vault—everything related to the monastery's history and regional surveys."

"Right away, sir."

"This is Miss Nassar. She and I will be working together for the next few weeks."

This time, rather than raise a brow, she smirked, knowing full well I'd baited her.

I'd chosen the room I asked be made ready for two reasons. First, while it was one of the monastery's original chambers, it had been expanded over time but still maintained its contemplative atmosphere. It had high ceilings with exposed beams, windows overlooking the loch, and walls that had heard centuries of prayers but now would witness something else entirely. Second, as was specified in the old architectural plans, it was adjacent to my own suite, connected by a door that hadn't been opened in decades.

"This is lovely," Leila said when I led her upstairs to see it. She set her bag down, then moved to look out the windows.

"When you're ready, my study is downstairs, second door on the right past the main staircase."

"I'll need an hour or so to prepare."

"Take your time," I said, leaving and heading to my own rooms to shower and change.

As I stood under the hot water, memories of Leila and me in the bath, her naked body relaxed against mine, played in a loop that included the sounds she'd made when we made love, the scrape of her nails on my back, and the hardest part, the way she'd sobbed when I held her in Dunravin's kitchen.

After dressing in jeans and a thick sweater to ward off the winter chill, I made my way downstairs to my study.

The room was perfect for our purposes—not the grand library with its soaring ceilings and thousands of volumes, but my private space where I handled estate business and the more discreet aspects of my work. It had a biometric access panel, large oak tables for spreading documents, and multiple exits, including the main door, French doors to the garden, and if you knew where to look, access to the old monastery passages.

I pulled out my mobile and rang Con.

"Tag." My best friend's voice came through clear. "How is Nightingale?"

"Making the best of a difficult situation."

"And you?"

"The same."

"Christ, mate. You're both idiots."

I didn't dare ask what he meant by that. If I did, I'd be in for a lengthy lecture I was not in the mood for. "I'm aware. Listen, are you and Lex available for a briefing tomorrow?"

"Of course. Lex has been eagerly awaiting your arrival."

"Are Ash, Sullivan, and Gus at Ashcroft?"

"Ash and Sullivan are, but Gus is in Edinburgh. I'm sure he can arrange to be back tomorrow."

"What about Renegade and Archon?"

"They're in London but can fly up with Viper. Do you want to fill me in on the short version?"

"McLaren's alive, Con. Or at least, someone with her exact knowledge and methods is active."

There was silence on the other end, then, "Bloody hell. If she survived that explosion—"

"Agreed. Which is why we need everyone here. Tomorrow."

"Roger that, and Tag?"

"Yeah?"

"Don't let Nightingale disappear again."

"I won't." Even if I had to lock her in the Blue Room and stand guard outside her door. Although knowing Leila, she'd find a way out through the windows or the old passages.

I checked in with Typhon first, then Viper. By the time I finished, Leila was standing in the doorway.

She'd changed into dark jeans and a burgundy sweater that brought out the gold flecks in her eyes. Her hair was still damp from the shower, falling in waves past her shoulders. She looked young and vulnerable and beautiful, and I had to force myself not to go to her, not to pull her into my arms and promise things I couldn't deliver.

"May I come in?"

"Of course. It's your operations center too."

She moved into the room, carrying her laptop and tablet, choosing the far end of the table—as far from where I stood as possible while remaining in the same room. The message was clear.

"If we're doing this," she said without looking at me, "we do it my way. I control the intelligence flow. You want to see something, you ask. No accessing my tablet, no going around me to get information. Understood?"

"I wouldn't dream of going around you."

She glanced up then, frowning at my smirk.

"And I need access to your historical archives. Everything about the estates, the tunnels, the connections between your family, Ash's, and Con's."

"The monastery vault has records going back five hundred years. They're yours."

When her eyes met mine and lingered, I wondered what she was thinking, what she might say.

"Talk to me, Nightingale," I finally said when she didn't speak.

"The investigation is our focus. Once we stop whatever McLaren and Janus are planning, I'm leaving."

"I understand."

"Do you?" She stood, moving to the window that overlooked the loch. The water was choppy today, wind-whipped and gray. "Because tomorrow, this place will be full of people who know us both. Con, who can read people better than anyone. Ash and Sullivan, who just found happiness and will notice our misery. Your team…"

"They care about the same thing I do. Namely, that you're safe."

She returned to the table without acknowledging what I said. "Do you want to see what I found about the tunnel networks, or should we wait for the others?"

"I'd love to," I said, standing beside her, once again wishing I could put my hands on her shoulders and simply *touch* her.

"I'm convinced these were never random smuggling routes," she said, pulling my mind back to the investigation. "They're infrastructure. Planned, maintained, and expanded over centuries."

There was a knock at the door that stood partially ajar, and I waved Douglas inside. He carried a large box that, when opened, revealed several books containing monastery records.

"What are those?" Leila asked.

"Glenshadow's history. We'll have to dig through them, but according to Sullivan, Fallon Wallace found maps showing tunnels that connect this estate to Ashcroft and Blackmoor, including information suggesting they date back to the Jacobite era."

"How fascinating," she said, reaching in to pull one of the heavy books from the box.

"Let me get that for you."

Leila shot me a look that made me laugh, and I held up both hands.

"Apologies. You're likely twice as strong as I am."

"And don't you forget it." When her eyes met mine, I caught the first sign of a glint.

We spent the next few hours looking through the books that Douglas continued delivering until darkness fell and Mrs. Murray delivered dinner to the study—stew, fresh bread, and wine neither of us touched. We ate in silence, the only sounds the crackling fire and rain against windows that reminded me so much of being at Dunravin.

"I should review more files," Leila said as the clock struck twenty-two hundred.

"You should rest. You barely slept last night."

She didn't look up from her tablet. "I'm fine, Tag. Stop hovering."

I wanted to argue, wanted to insist, but I refrained. "I'll be here if you need anything."

"I won't."

The dismissal was clear. She gathered her things and left without another word.

I remained in my study, alone, looking at the books stacked on the table. Tomorrow, the team would arrive and we'd dive into the investigation.

I reached for my bottle of whiskey when the bitter irony of it all hit me. I'd won the battle—she was here, working with me. But in the end, I'd lose the war. And the enemy was myself.

9

Nightingale

The first thing I did when I entered the bedroom—
aka my prison cell—was draft a message to Kestrel. If
anyone could help me disappear, this asset could. Yes,
I'd signed up for this heartache when I agreed to come
to Glenshadow, but even temporarily was harder than
I'd anticipated.

Tag had been crystal clear—what happened at
Dunravin ended at Dunravin. No negotiations, no
exceptions. He'd drawn his line like a sniper's bullet,
and I was the one bleeding out from it.

Request relocation assistance.

The response came within minutes. *Negative. Too
much risk. Unknown hostiles tracked you to London
safe house. Motivation unclear. Stay put.*

My jaw clenched. *I extracted myself from Edinburgh
alone. Left London safe house before your asset
arrived. I don't need protection.*

The cursor blinked for longer this time before Kestrel's response appeared. *Glasgow required Viper's intervention. London required MacTaggert's. Pattern suggests escalating danger. Disappearing now would be a mistake.*

Then I'll disappear without your help. I deleted the message rather than send it. First, announcing my departure, given Kestrel wouldn't help, would be stupid. Second, the asset had resources I needed, contacts that could make vanishing easier. Burning that bridge out of frustration wouldn't be prudent. Instead, I powered down the tablet and set it aside.

I lay against the pillows, but sleep felt impossible. My body remembered things my mind was trying to forget. The weight of Tag's hands on my hips. The heat of his mouth against my throat. The way he'd whispered my name like a prayer when he was inside me. Three nights of desperate lovemaking that had rewritten every cell in my body, and now, I was supposed to pretend none of it had happened.

My thoughts drifted to his parents. His mother's abandonment. His father basically doing the same thing except with alcohol. Tag had painted them as monsters who'd destroyed each other, but were they really so different from us? We were managing our own destruction quite efficiently—his through denial, mine through compliance.

Who could tell me more about them? The housekeeper had likely been with the family for years. If so, she'd have known them both. But asking her directly wouldn't be fair. Not to mention she might alert Tag that I had. Maybe I could figure out a way to approach it casually. Test the waters first.

When a floorboard creaked in the hallway, I went completely still, every nerve ending alive. Footsteps—I knew that stride better than my own heartbeat. Tag had stopped right outside my door.

My heart hammered against my ribs as I stared at the door handle, willing it to turn. *Please,* I thought desperately. *Please just come in. Tell me you were wrong. Tell me you can't do this, either.*

One second. Two. Three. Each one stretched like an eternity until the footsteps resumed.

Anger and disappointment settled on my chest, and I released a breath I hadn't realized I was holding. Coward. We both were.

After staring at the ceiling for several minutes, I knew sleep wouldn't come any time soon. I threw off the covers and padded to the windows, examining them properly for the first time. I was on the second floor, overlooking the loch. The windows were old, with thick glass and heavy frames. They opened, but not wide enough for a person to fit through. Even if they did, it was a straight drop to the stone below. No convenient ivy or drainpipes like in novels.

I moved to the other door in the room—not the main entrance, but a side door I'd noticed earlier. The handle didn't budge when I tried it. Locked from the other side, most likely.

For a moment, I considered picking it. It would be easy enough to do. But what if it led to Tag's room? Breaking in and finding him asleep or, worse, waking him up and having to explain wouldn't solve anything. It would only make the emotional agony worse.

I returned to bed, pulling the blankets up to my chin despite the room being warm enough. Tomorrow, the team would arrive and I'd be forced to stand beside Tag like none of this was killing me. I'd have to be Special Agent Nassar, not the woman who'd given her virginity to a man who'd warned her they had no future.

Eventually, exhaustion won over anxiety, and I drifted into a restless sleep, dreaming of locked doors and footsteps that didn't walk away.

I'd barely finished dressing the next morning when a knock came at my door. Not Tag's—this was sharper, more authoritative.

"Come in," I called, smoothing my hair back into a tight bun.

Viper entered, her MI6 polish intact despite the early hour. Bellamy Hall had the kind of presence that commanded rooms without effort, and even in Tag's ancestral home, she moved like she owned the place.

"We need to discuss your status." She closed the door behind her. "The others are gathering in Tag's study, but I wanted to speak with you privately first."

My stomach tightened. "Has there been a development?"

"Your arrangement with MI6 is ending. You'll return to Unit 23's direct command for the remainder of the Labyrinth investigation."

"I see."

"MacTaggert will resume as your handler."

No. Please no.

I steeled my expression through sheer force of will. "May I ask why the change?"

Viper moved to the window, gazing out at the loch. "The inter-agency loan was always meant to be temporary. With the investigation centralizing here and the full team mobilizing, MI6 no longer needs to serve as intermediary."

My mind raced back to the London safe house, to Viper appearing in my doorway that night. She'd been testing me, evaluating my commitment to the mission. Had my swift departure soon after she left triggered this?

"I understand," I managed, though understanding and accepting were vastly different things.

Her gaze sharpened. "Is there an issue I should be made aware of?"

"I—" I stopped and recalibrated. What could I say that would explain my obvious hesitation? "I've appreciated the autonomy of working with MI6. Returning to Unit 23's structure will be an adjustment."

She raised a brow. "You *are* a Unit 23 operative, unless your intention is to leave that role."

"No, ma'am. It is not."

"Good." She moved toward the door, then paused. "The investigation is entering a critical phase. It will require everyone to perform at their highest level. I cannot imagine any reason to anticipate you wouldn't."

"Of course not."

"Typhon should be arriving shortly. The full briefing will begin then." She opened the door, then glanced back. "Oh, and, Nassar? The gap between you leaving my presence at the safe house and MacTaggert finding you at King's Cross—I trust we won't see a repeat." She motioned to the hallway. "Ready to join the others?"

"I'll be along in a minute."

She nodded once, then walked out. When the door clicked behind her, I sank onto the bed, my legs unsteady. Every mission, every briefing, every debrief—I'd be forced to work by Tag's side. There was no refusing orders, no explaining why this arrangement was torture without revealing the very thing that would compromise us both.

The irony wasn't lost on me. I'd asked Kestrel for escape assistance, and instead, the chains had just gotten tighter.

When I entered Tag's study, where the meeting would take place, our eyes connected. He stood near the far wall and had been studying a map. Heat raced through my veins despite every reminder I'd made to myself that we were back to Obsidian and Nightingale, not that I heard his code name used that often anymore. I looked away, but when I glanced back, he was still watching me.

He strode across the room, in my direction, his eyes never leaving mine. "Mrs. Murray mentioned you hadn't eaten breakfast."

"I wasn't hungry."

His hand rose toward my face, a gesture so familiar from Dunravin that my body leaned toward him instinctively. Then he dropped it, and I stepped away, putting the table between us before taking a seat at the opposite end from where he'd been standing.

As soon as I'd opened my laptop and loaded my notes for the briefing, a helicopter's distinctive thrum announced Typhon's arrival. When he entered minutes later, urgency marked his expression. He greeted Tag and Viper as the others entered the room and took their seats.

"Thank you all for being here," Tag said, looking at those assembled—Con and Lex, Ash and Sullivan, Gus, Renegade, and Archon. "Nightingale will be briefing us on recent intelligence regarding Project Labyrinth."

I stood, pulling up my files on a digital display that lowered from the ceiling. Every eye in the room tracked to the screen, then back to me. I'd done hundreds of briefings, but this one felt different. Maybe because Tag was watching.

"Before we discuss what I found in Damascus and the developments since then, Sullivan, would you mind giving us an overview of how the investigation into Tower-Meridian began and what happened subsequently?"

"Of course." She stood and cleared her throat. "My investigation into Eric Weber began months ago at a charity event in Edinburgh. While he wasn't in attendance, the announcement of his billion-dollar donation stunned those who were—myself included. The numbers didn't add up, and the more I dug, the worse it looked."

Manifests appeared on the screen. "Tower-Meridian's records showed significant irregularities—humanitarian aid shipments arriving thirty percent lighter than their departure weight, temperature logs with gaps of several hours, tracking systems that went dark for extended periods. My theory was that they were shipping something else entirely, possibly weapons components disguised as medical equipment."

She paused, her expression darkening. "As you all know, at the end of December, I was abducted from the Ashcroft library by Fallon Wallace and taken into the tunnels beneath the estate. During that abduction, I learned that Fallon Wallace and Eric Weber were the same person—a woman operating under a male alias." Sullivan stopped and looked over at Ash, and her cheeks flushed. "She was killed during my rescue."

She sat down, and all eyes returned to me.

"The day after Sullivan's rescue, I sent an encrypted file from Damascus." I pulled up the relevant documents. "A coup had occurred in Syria—the president fled to Russia, rebel forces took control, and I found myself in significant danger. The file I sent contained intelligence I'd found buried in encrypted communications. It confirmed what Sullivan just said—that Eric Weber was an alias used by Fallon Wallace. I also learned her code name was Chimera. More critically, it revealed that Tower-Meridian intended to sell autonomous integrated weapon systems—or AIWS—to Russia, China, and potentially other nations."

I let that information settle before continuing. "But there was something else in those encrypted files. Evidence suggesting that someone within MI6 was connected to Project Labyrinth. Coded communications that, once we broke them down, showed someone on the inside of SIS had been feeding information to the Labyrinth network."

I paused, glancing between Typhon and Viper.

"We spent nearly two weeks analyzing the Damascus intelligence," I continued. "Cross-referencing communications, tracking information flows, building profiles.

We narrowed it down to a handful of possibilities, then zeroed in on one name: Malcolm Bennett.”

I glanced at Lex and Con. “Viper made the decision to send Bennett to work with your team investigating Orlov. The theory was that if he was the mole, he might make a move. Lex, would you update everyone on what happened at the facility?”

She stood, her expression somber. “Con and I had been tracking Viktor Orlov—whom everyone believed dead—first to Aberdeenshire, then to a facility near Inverness. Bennett joined our team mid-January.”

Surveillance images appeared on the display. “The investigation became complicated when we discovered Evelyn McLaren had been involved with Orlov’s neural interface research for at least two decades. What we eventually pieced together was that Bennett and McLaren were working together to sabotage Orlov’s system from within after learning he intended to weaponize it for mass devastation.”

She glanced down at Con, who reached up to squeeze her hand. “During our final assault on the facility, McLaren and Bennett’s countermeasure caused the neural interface to overload. The resulting explosion destroyed the facility and the AIWS prototype. Bennett was killed in the crossfire, and while Orlov survived, he has apparent severe cognitive damage—he's either unable or unwilling to communicate beyond basic responses. McLaren's body was never recovered from the explosion."

Lex sat down, and I pulled up the next set of files.

"After the explosion, I continued analyzing the intelligence I'd gathered in Syria." I shared the evidence I'd already presented to Tag—the four categories suggesting McLaren wasn't dead—communications using her unique terminology, financial transfers through Cyprus and Malta, reactivated cells with her tradecraft, and technical signatures matching her neural interface work. "What I found suggests that Dr. McLaren survived."

Typhon's head snapped up, his eyes narrowing.

"The communications reference someone called 'the Architect,'" I continued. "Based on everything I've found, I believe that's McLaren. However, she's not operating independently. There are references to her communicating with someone about moving into phase two, strongly suggesting that she is not Janus."

I paused. "Which brings us to what Tag and I discovered at Dunravin Castle. Extensive, functional tunnel networks—far more sophisticated than anyone suspected. Multiple passages, some leading toward the North Sea, others connecting inland.

"Combined with what we know exists beneath Ashcroft, Blackmoor, and Glenshadow—estates Fallon showed particular interest in—and the well-documented passages in Edinburgh, a clear picture emerges. The stone construction blocks standard electronic surveillance. Historical estate privileges prevent government inspection. Whoever is behind Project Labyrinth may be exploiting these tunnel systems for covert movement of AIWS components."

I looked around the room. "Tower-Meridian has all but collapsed since Fallon Wallace's death, but Project Labyrinth continues. We need to identify Janus, to locate McLaren if she's alive, and we need to determine where components are being manufactured and how they're being distributed before the next phase of Labyrinth is deployed."

The room was silent for several seconds, everyone processing.

Typhon cleared his throat. "Before we discuss the next steps, I have a related update. Clive Edwards, the former executive editor of investigations for the Crown Herald News Agency, was arrested three days ago on charges relating to his association with Fallon Wallace. They include conspiracy, treason, and accessory to attempted murder. He's cooperating fully in exchange for a reduced sentence."

I looked at Sullivan. Clive was her uncle—one who'd betrayed his own family when she got too close to the truth. Her expression remained steeled, but I saw Ash's hand find hers under the table.

"Anything else to add?" I asked her quietly.

"We can move on," she responded.

Typhon stood, commanding the room's attention. "There's another matter I want to address. We're bringing two new operatives into this investigation. Both are MI6 assets with specialized capabilities."

As he spoke, I felt the mobile in my pocket buzz with a specific alert, indicating I'd received a message from Kestrel. I silenced it while Typhon continued.

"The first is Oliver Morse, code name Vanguard. MI6 operative with extensive experience in the Middle East. He speaks Arabic and French fluently, and has contacts throughout Syrian military and intelligence circles."

Typhon's eyes found mine. "If I'm not mistaken, Nightingale, you and Vanguard worked together previously."

"Yes, sir," I responded.

"The second is Ophelia Okonkwo, code name Prima," Typhon continued. "Her father is Sir Anthony Okonkwo, British-Nigerian career diplomat. She was raised in embassies across three continents, speaks eight languages, and is trained in psychological operations. She has extensive contacts throughout Eastern Europe and, coincidentally, met Viktor Orlov at a Moscow embassy function two years ago. Her FSB asset recently resurfaced, claiming to have Labyrinth intelligence, though that hasn't been confirmed yet."

"I can personally vouch for both Prima and Vanguard," Viper added. "They are exemplary and highly professional operatives."

The way she looked at me when she said it made my paranoia flare. Was that a pointed comment?

From the corner of my eye, I saw Con quietly check his phone, then slip it back into his pocket. His expression didn't change, but something shifted in his posture, making me think he'd also heard from Kestrel.

"Prima just landed in Glasgow," Typhon said, glancing at his mobile. "She and Vanguard should arrive within the hour."

I stood. "This would be a good time for a break, then. We can regroup once they're here and discuss investigation strategies."

Typhon nodded. "Agreed. Reconvene in one hour."

As those in the room began to disperse, Tag moved toward me, but I was already gathering my laptop and heading for the door.

I needed to see what Kestrel had sent. And I needed to see it before anyone—especially Tag—could ask questions I wasn't ready to answer.

I found Con in the corridor just outside the study, staring at his mobile.

"You got it too?" I whispered.

He looked up. "Let's take this outside."

After we'd walked several paces from the castle's entrance, I pulled up the encrypted message.

It was brief—exactly Kestrel's style.

PRIORITY INTEL:

Edinburgh: Gallery district financial transactions (Cyprus/Malta accounts)

Teesport: Shipping anomalies, container diversions

Northern Highlands: Thermal activity detected Inverness region

Mediterranean financial networks active.

Recommend immediate investigation.

Con stared at the screen, his expression shifting to recognition before he looked up at me. "Lex and I had eyes on a specific gallery in Edinburgh when we were tracking Orlov—the Imperial. We couldn't prove anything then, but we suspected money laundering. The clientele didn't match legitimate art collectors."

"Kestrel's intel confirms current activity," I said, studying the details.

"There was a private members' club by the same name involved. We were able to listen into one conversation before almost being discovered. We overheard things about a consortium, a developer, and integration timelines. We suspected they were discussing Orlov, but like the money laundering, we couldn't confirm it then." Con tapped the screen. "If Kestrel's pointing us back to Edinburgh's gallery district, my guess is that these locations are active again."

"Which means the network didn't collapse after Inverness."

"No. It reorganized."

I checked my watch. "We have approximately forty-five minutes to sift through this and craft a plan to address it."

"Right. Library?"

I was about to follow him inside when Tag approached.

"Hey," he said.

"Hi."

"Got a minute?" He motioned to the bench.

"Actually, I do not."

"Please."

I folded my arms. "What do you want, Tag?"

"What did Typhon mean about you and Vanguard?"

My eyes scrunched. "What are you talking about?"

"His reference."

"Do you mean him saying we *worked* together previously?"

"I got the impression there was more to it than that."

"I can't do this." When I spun around, he caught my arm.

"Just tell me," he demanded in a tone that set me off.

"You want to know what happened? We had a mad, passionate love affair in Syria that we both insisted end the moment we set foot out of the country," I spat at him.

"I obviously know you didn't."

"Then maybe you should mind your own bloody business," I seethed.

"I can't. I care about you and—"

I laughed. Heartily. Then turned away. "Not another word, *Obsidian*. We're done here. Actually, we were finished the moment we set foot out of Dunravin."

I stalked through the front door, down the corridor, and joined Con in the library.

"Everything okay?" he asked.

"Fine," I snapped, pulling out a chair. He took the seat beside me.

"I had Kestrel clarify a few things while I was waiting," he began. "The most important is that this intel requires immediate investigation. Multiple active sites, coordinated activity. We cannot afford to delay."

I forced myself to focus, to compartmentalize. Tag didn't matter right now. The mission did. "Then, we need to figure out what we're dealing with."

"Three distinct areas," Con said, pulling up his phone. "Edinburgh art market—high-value transactions in the past seventy-two hours, Cyprus accounts active. That connects to the financial transactions Gus identified previously—art galleries as potential money laundering fronts for Labyrinth."

"The second is Teesport," I continued, my voice steadier now. "Shipping anomalies, containers being rerouted. Weight discrepancies that match the Tower-Meridian patterns." I waited for questions, and when there weren't any, I moved on to the next area Kestrel mentioned.

"Finally, the Northern Highlands—the Inverness region. Thermal activity detected, recent movement." I paused, lowering my voice. "Dunravin is in that region. Tag and I found extensive tunnel systems there."

Con's expression shifted. "You think the thermal signatures could be coming from there?"

"It's possible." I glanced in the direction of the door and lowered my voice. "Dunravin is Renegade's family estate. We can't bring this up in the briefing without evidence. It would put him in an impossible position."

Con nodded. "Agreed. We keep it general during the presentation—just the Inverness region. But whoever investigates the Northern Highlands needs to know where to start looking." He studied his phone again. "And the financial trail—Malta and Cyprus networks active. Art sales funding operations through multiple dealers."

"We need teams at each location," I said.

Con nodded. "Edinburgh makes sense for Lex and me since we already know the lay of the land."

"Sullivan and Ash for Teesport. Sullivan's investigation started there."

"Archon, Vanguard, and Prima for the Northern Highlands," I suggested. "I can brief them separately after the meeting concludes."

"And Gus with Renegade for the financial networks."

"That leaves Tag and me," I reminded him.

"Right. Here's what I propose. When the meeting reconvenes, we present this together. It may be that it'll become obvious where the two of you are needed the most."

There was something about his statement that didn't sit right with me. However, given we were short on time, I'd wait to see how it played out once the team was gathered.

"Typhon and Viper will likely want to make the final deployment decisions," he added.

"Sure. Makes sense. Also, Vanguard and Prima will need an overview when they arrive. I'll handle that as quickly as possible."

"I have a question for you. You can decline to answer if you wish."

Oh, God, something about Tag? I would definitely turn him down. "Go ahead."

"Kestrel."

My eyes widened. "In regard to?"

"How did you, I mean…"

"How did Kestrel become *my* asset?"

"Basically, yes."

"Idris." The truth wasn't that simple. Kestrel had contacted me shortly after I joined Unit 23, with intel regarding Labyrinth. The references were vague initially, but most of what I'd been able to piece together in my brother's encrypted files was with the asset's help. Eventually, I'd accepted that Kestrel was just another person Idris had tasked with looking out for me. It was a curse as much as a blessing.

Con stood, then paused. "One more thing before we join the others. I just want to say—Tag is struggling. I won't pretend he's not. But he's worth the fight. Worth taking the risk."

"I know he is." My voice was steadier than I expected it to be. "But he's not willing to fight his past. And I can't do it for him."

Con held my gaze for a long moment, then nodded. "Let's go brief the team."

10

Tag

Con found me in my study before the meeting reconvened.

"I received intel about activity in the Northern Highlands," he began, closing the door behind him.

I looked up from the briefings spread across my desk. "Dunravin?"

"Most likely. The reports indicate thermal signatures, and the location fits with what you and Nightingale found there. However, we're keeping it vague during the briefing. 'Northern Highlands near Inverness'—nothing more specific."

I raised a brow. "You and Nightingale?"

"That's right. We received the same intelligence."

"And your intention is to protect Renegade."

"Exactly. If he thinks his family estate is compromised, it becomes a distraction. We confirm it's Dunravin first, then we read him in. Nightingale and I discussed it—this is the right approach."

I nodded slowly. The logic was sound. "Agreed. Anything else?"

"We'll cover it when the team reconvenes."

I didn't like the sound of that, but given there wasn't much time between then and now, I acquiesced.

"As to your question. I want to talk to you about your relationship with Nightingale."

"It's none of your business."

"Wrong. As your lifelong best friend, it's as much my concern as you are."

"Not now. I'm busy."

"Drinking yourself into oblivion isn't busy." He crossed to the sideboard, pouring himself two fingers. "It's pathetic."

"Fuck off, Con."

"No." He settled into the chair across from my desk, still holding both his glass and the bottle of whiskey. "You told me you and Nightingale had a friends-with-benefits arrangement."

My hand stilled on my own glass. "So?"

Rather than in front of me, he set the whiskey bottle on the table beside him. "It was a lie."

I should've known he'd figure it out. Con had watched me lie to targets, to assets, to enemies across three continents. But never to him. Not until Nightingale.

"What's really going on?"

I stared into my glass but remained silent.

"You're both miserable. Why?"

The question hung between us. I could deflect. But Con wasn't going to let this go.

"My parents," I finally said.

Con leaned in his chair, waiting.

"I can't become them. I won't put her through what they went through. What they did to each other—" I stopped. "You remember."

"Of course I do. I've known you since we were eight. I watched it all."

"Then, you know why—"

"What I know is you're terrified." He leaned forward. "But you're not them, Tag."

"How can you be sure?"

"Because they never tried. They gave up at the first sign of trouble and turned it into warfare."

I knocked back the rest of my drink and stood to reach for the bottle, but Con's hand got there first.

"Talk to me."

"There's nothing to say."

"Bollocks." He poured me another measure anyway. One finger, not three. "Because she's Idris' sister? Or because you're in love with her?"

My throat closed, and I couldn't respond.

Con's face changed. The frustration bled away, replaced by something I liked even less—understanding. "So what happened at Dunravin?"

"Nothing that matters now."

"Try again," he said as he poured more whiskey into my glass.

I stared at the amber liquid, wondering how many more drinks it would take before I stopped seeing the hurt in her expression. That I'd caused.

"I slept with her." The confession scraped out. "Multiple times. Then I told her it couldn't continue once we left."

"Jesus, Tag."

"I know."

"Do you?" Con stood, pacing to the window. "Because from where I'm standing, you're making this worse for both of you."

"I ended it before—"

"Before what? Before you could be happy?" He spun around. "Your parents' marriage wasn't everyone's fate. Mine weren't much better. But they never loved each other, Tag. Yours did—at first. Then they gave up and turned vicious."

"They destroyed each other. I'm protecting her—"

"From what? From having someone who actually loves her?" His laugh was bitter. "You and Nightingale have fought alongside each other for three years. She's proven herself in ways most operatives never will. She's not some society girl who'll run at first trouble."

Like my mother had been.

"She deserves better than—"

"Than someone who loves her enough to be terrified of losing her? That's everyone worth having, you idiot. The thought of losing Lex scares the hell out of me—" He stopped and regrouped. "But I'd rather have that fear than live without her."

I had no response to that.

"You're so terrified of becoming them, you're creating a different destruction. One where you're both miserable but you get to pretend it's noble."

"At least she can find happiness with someone else."

"You'll be okay with it if she finds solace with another man?"

"She'll get over me."

"Will she? Or will she spend the rest of her life settling for men who don't make her feel what you do? Men who are safe because they don't matter?"

I looked away. Out the window, toward the loch, where the afternoon light caught the water that was as peaceful as it was deceptive.

"You don't want to turn into your parents? Then, do things differently. Don't give up. Especially on her."

"I can't give her what she needs."

"You mean you won't. There's a difference."

The distinctive thrum of helicopter rotors cut through the air. We both turned toward the window.

"That'll be Vanguard and Prima." Con stood and walked to the door, then paused. "Lex asked me once if I thought love was worth the risk. I said yes. Because the alternative—living without her—that's not living at all." His hand hit the doorframe. "You're not

living either, mate. You're just surviving. And drag-
ging Nightingale down with you."

After the door closed behind him, I sat alone with
the bottle and the truth I couldn't face.

Con was wrong. He had to be. Because if he
wasn't—if I was destroying us both for nothing—then
every wall I'd built, every promise I'd made to myself,
every reason I'd pushed her away meant nothing.

I stood at the window, watching as the chopper's
rotors slowed and two figures emerged.

"They're here," Renegade said from the doorway
as I poured one last round in my glass. "Should I let
everyone know it's okay to come back in?"

"Sure."

The study filled quickly—Con and Lex took their
previous seats, as did Ash and Sullivan. Gus claimed
the window seat while Renegade and Archon flanked
the door like sentries. Nightingale entered last, choosing the seat farthest from me.

Our eyes met for half a second, showing heat and
hurt in equal measure. Then she looked away.

Typhon appeared with Viper, followed by
the newcomers.

Vanguard came in first. The man had sandy-brown hair and the build of someone who spent more time in gyms than cockpits. How old had Typhon said he was? Twenty-eight? Fuck. He was young, uncomplicated, everything I wasn't.

"Now that we're all here," Typhon said, "I'll let Vanguard and Prima introduce themselves properly before we continue."

Morse stepped forward with an easy confidence. "Oliver Morse. Most people call me Ollie." His eyes swept the room, cataloging and assessing.

When his gaze landed on Nightingale, his expression transformed.

"Leila!" The warmth in his voice made my jaw clench. "I didn't realize you'd be here. This is brilliant."

She stood, professional but not cold. Not the ice she'd given me outside. "Vanguard. Good to see you."

Code name rather than first, like he'd used with her. Did that mean she was establishing a professional distance or trying to hide a more personal relationship between them?

He crossed to her without hesitation, and they embraced. Nothing inappropriate—just the ease of two people who'd worked together before.

"What's it been, three months since we were last together?"

"More like six," she said, smiling.

"Three days would've been too long," he said, winking.

The whiskey in my stomach turned to acid.

"Nightingale's one of the best I've worked with," Morse said to the room, though his attention stayed on her. "Brilliant under fire. Keeps her head when everyone else is losing theirs."

Con cleared his throat, and I realized my hand had tightened into a fist.

Okonkwo introduced herself but otherwise kept it brief, then stepped back, clearly content to observe.

But Morse stayed near Nightingale.

My Nightingale.

Except she wasn't mine. Not anymore. I'd made sure of that.

"Right then," I said, my voice sharper than intended. "Shall we get to work?"

"I was about to suggest that I brief Vanguard and Prima on current intelligence," Nightingale said.

"Go ahead," Typhon responded.

She moved to stand beside the tactical display, and naturally—of course—Vanguard followed, positioning himself close enough that their shoulders nearly touched as she pulled up files.

"I'll give you the short version," she began. "Project Labyrinth is a weapons network trafficking AIWS. Selective EMP technology with neural interface capabilities. The system can disable all electronics in a region while protecting specific signatures."

Vanguard leaned in to study the display, his hand bracing on the table, mere inches from hers. "Christ. That's worse than what we encountered in the Baltic."

"Significantly worse." She pulled up schematics. "The woman who ran Tower-Meridian—Fallon Wallace—was killed in December, but the network continues. We believe Evelyn McLaren survived the explosion at Orlov's facility and is still active, working for someone with the code name Janus."

"Any idea who that is?" Prima asked.

Nightingale's jaw tightened. "Not yet."

Her hand gestured at the maps of Scotland as she walked them through the tunnel networks. Vanguard's attention never left her face, making the anger inside me build.

"Amazing work," he said when she finished. "Same Leila I remember—ten steps ahead of everyone else."

The familiarity in his tone made my teeth grind.

"Right." Con stood. "If that about covers it, Nightingale and I have urgent information to share with everyone."

She met his eyes, nodded once, then moved to stand beside him.

"We received intel during the break," Con began, pulling up a map with three markers. "Multiple locations showing coordinated activity—Edinburgh art market, Teesport, and the Northern Highlands near Inverness."

"All active simultaneously," Nightingale added. "Which suggests Labyrinth is ramping up operations."

"We're proposing immediate team deployments based on expertise and existing investigation threads," Con said. "Lex and I will take Edinburgh—we've been there before, surveilling the Imperial Gallery during the Orlov investigation. We know the area, know the locations. We just didn't have proof of activity then. Kestrel's intel changes that. Ash and

Sullivan will handle Teesport. Vanguard, Prima, and Archon for the Northern Highlands. Gus, Nightingale, and Renegade on financial networks tracking the Mediterranean connections."

I watched relief flicker across Nightingale's face. She'd avoided being paired with me.

"One moment," Typhon said, standing. "There's another angle we need to address that isn't in Kestrel's immediate intelligence—the Tarbert estates. Glenshadow, Blackmoor, and Ashcroft."

He pulled up maps showing all three properties. "Wallace was fixated on these specific locations, where we know extensive tunnel systems exist."

"What are you proposing?" Viper asked.

"We need to understand why she targeted these properties specifically," Typhon said. "What was she planning to move through those tunnels? What infrastructure was she building?" His eyes moved to me, then to Nightingale. "MacTaggert has access to all three estates. Nightingale has the deepest knowledge of Wallace's operational patterns from the Damascus intelligence."

The relief on Nightingale's face vanished, replaced by tension.

"And remaining at Glenshadow provides the necessary security," Viper added, her gaze steady on Nightingale, "while unknown hostiles are still tracking you."

Leila's jaw tightened, but she couldn't argue with the logic.

"Map the tunnel systems," Typhon ordered, looking between us. "Review Wallace's documentation. Determine what she intended. Understanding her strategy might reveal what Labyrinth is doing now."

The room was silent for a beat.

"One more adjustment," Typhon continued. "Archon stays here."

Archon's head came up. "Sir?"

"You'll provide additional security for Nightingale while the investigation proceeds. After what happened in London, I'm not taking chances with her safety. Vanguard and Prima can handle the northern corridor as a two-person team. Questions?" He scanned the room, but no one spoke up. "Good. Teams will deploy tomorrow morning. By then, transport will be in place. Tonight, we finalize operational details."

When everyone stood, Vanguard crossed back to Nightingale.

"Take care of yourself," he said quietly, but not enough that I couldn't hear. "And if you need anything—"

"I'll be fine," she said.

"I know you will be. You always are." He touched her shoulder. "But the offer stands."

Then he was gone, heading out with the others.

Archon approached me as the room emptied. "Boss, if I'm staying at Glenshadow, I should probably sort where I should bunk. Is there—"

"Find Mrs. Murray. Have her set you up in the west wing."

"Appreciated." He paused. "For what it's worth, Nightingale's damn good."

I looked across the room to where she stood, gathering her laptop. Her spine was rigid, and her movements controlled. "She's better than good."

Archon wisely left without another word.

Needing a moment away from the noise, from watching Vanguard position himself near Nightingale, from pretending I was fine with any of this, I found Gus in the library, cross-referencing financial data with shipping manifests that were spread across the large table.

"Found the connection yet?" I asked, dropping into the chair across from him.

"Getting close. This shell-company matrix is clever, but not clever enough." He looked up, studying my face. "You look like hell, mate."

"Long few days."

"Nightingale?"

Of course he'd know. Gus always knew. "It's complicated."

"It usually is with women worth having." He returned to his data, but added quietly, "Con's worried about you. So am I."

"I'm fine."

"Sure you are." He made a notation on one of the manifests. "Just remember—you lot pulled me through finding out about my family. Let us do the same for you."

I didn't respond, but the offer sat there between us, solid as the friendship that had weathered three decades.

"For what it's worth," Gus said, still not looking up, "watching Ash nearly lose Sullivan taught me something. Being scared isn't a good enough reason not to try."

He went back to his numbers, and I sat there, wondering when all my friends had gotten so bloody wise.

While Mrs. Murray had outdone herself with the preparation of roasted meats, root vegetables, and fresh bread, dinner was torture as I sat at the head of the table, watching Nightingale laugh and converse with Vanguard.

She'd chosen a seat halfway down the table, and he'd taken the one beside her without hesitation.

"This is excellent," Lex said from my right, her voice carrying the forced brightness of someone trying to fill uncomfortable silence. "Tag, you'll have to give Mrs. Murray our compliments."

I managed a nod but reached for my glass.

Water. Con had switched it when I wasn't looking. The bloody bastard.

"The tunnel networks are more extensive than I expected," Vanguard said, continuing whatever conversation I'd missed. "From what you showed us, some of those passages could run for miles."

"The Jacobites knew what they were doing." Nightingale's voice carried the easy confidence of someone discussing her expertise. "They built to last."

Professional. Competent. It was a conversation I should've been part of. Instead, I watched them talk. Watched the way Vanguard hung on her every word.

"Tag?" Gus's voice cut through my spiral. "Thoughts on the Aberdeenshire coordinates?"

I forced my attention back. "What about them?"

"Whether we should prioritize them over the Inverness area."

"Ask Nightingale. She compiled the intelligence."

Her eyes met mine briefly, then she looked away.

"The Aberdeenshire sites show more recent activity," she said to Gus. "Inverness is cold after the explosion."

The meal dragged on. Sullivan discussed shipping manifests with Ash. Lex and Gus debated financial tracking methods. Renegade and Archon compared notes on equipment checks. It was all normal operational conversation that should've held my attention.

Instead, I watched Vanguard lean closer to Nightingale when she spoke. Watched her tuck a strand of hair behind her ear. Watched her be the version of herself she'd been at Dunravin—relaxed, genuine, and present.

With someone else.

"We should head out," Con eventually said, pushing back from the table. "Long day tomorrow."

Others followed his lead. Ash and Sullivan gathered their things while Gus checked his mobile for updated intelligence.

"Brilliant meal," Vanguard said to Mrs. Murray as she cleared the plates. "Thank you."

He had manners. Of course he did.

"I should get going as well." He stood, then turned to Nightingale. "I hope it won't be too long before we see each other again."

"We both have our assignments." Her smile was polite. "But I'm sure our paths will cross."

"Until then." He touched her shoulder briefly, further infuriating me enough that I wanted to put my fist through the wall.

The front hall filled with goodbyes and final instructions. Con caught my eye as he and Lex headed for the door. His look spoke louder than words—*don't do anything stupid.*

Too late for that.

Silence settled over Glenshadow like a shroud as the house emptied. Ash's Range Rover disappeared down the drive first, carrying him, Sullivan, and Gus.

Then Con's with Lex, Vanguard, and Prima. Typhon and Viper left too, although by then, I'd stopped paying attention.

"Need anything else tonight, boss?" Archon asked.

"Get some rest," I said, hating that I sounded like a man twelve years older than him. Than Nightingale.

When he retreated, I stood alone in the hall. The grandfather clock ticked, and the wind rattled the ancient windows. Somewhere upstairs, Nightingale was probably getting ready for bed.

In the room next to mine.

Connected by a door that hadn't been opened in decades.

I headed for my study and poured whiskey despite Con's warning, despite knowing it would only make things worse.

The thoughts I'd been holding back all evening crashed through the barriers.

She was no longer a virgin. Because of me.

Maybe she'd explore now. With others. Men who wouldn't push her away after.

I'd opened that door. Shown her what her body could feel. Then slammed it shut and told her to forget.

What right did I have to want her to stay celibate? To pine for a man who'd rejected her?

None.

But the thought of another man touching her the way I had—

The glass hit the desk harder than intended.

She deserved happiness. Deserved someone who could offer her tomorrow and all the tomorrows after. Someone who wasn't terrified of becoming his parents. Someone who hadn't promised her dead brother to keep her safe.

Safe. That's what I'd told myself. But Con was right—I was destroying us both while calling it protection.

Movement caught my eye in the hallway. A figure headed toward the library.

Nightingale.

My feet were moving before I'd made a conscious decision. Out of the study. Down the corridor. The whiskey made everything sharper and duller at the same time—edges too bright, thoughts too slow.

I caught up with her in the alcove just before the library entrance.

"Leila."

She spun around. Even in the dim light, I could see her expression shift from surprise to wariness.

"What are you doing out here?" I asked.

"Going to the library. What are you doing?"

Following you. Stalking you like some pathetic drunk who can't accept that he threw away the best thing in his life.

"Making sure you're all right."

Her laugh was sharp. "Now, you care about making sure I'm all right?"

The accusation landed true. I stepped closer. She stepped back.

"Don't." Her voice carried a warning.

I should've listened.

11

Nightingale

No matter how many times I turned over or punched the pillow, I wasn't able to sleep.

Eventually, I threw the covers off and put a jumper on over my tank top, planning to visit the library and get some work done.

As I headed downstairs, I thought about how quiet the castle was now that the rest of the team had left. I even assumed that other than me, and probably Tag, everyone else was asleep.

As soon as I reached the alcove near the library entrance, I heard a footstep, then my name.

"Leila."

I spun around when Tag emerged from the shadows. The smell of whiskey hit me first—sharp and peaty, clinging to him like he'd bathed in it rather than just drunk it. His movements were too measured, deliberate in the way of someone trying very hard not to appear drunk, and his eyes struggled to focus on my face.

"What are you doing out here?" His words weren't slurred, but the edges were soft.

"Going to the library. What are you doing?"

He moved closer, cutting off my path to the library entrance. "Making sure you're all right."

"Don't," I whispered, taking a step away.

His hand caught my wrist when he reached for me before I could skirt around him. "I can't stop thinking about you. About him."

"Him?"

"Vanguard." The name came out rough, almost accusatory, like I'd done something wrong by sitting next to the man at dinner. "The way he looked at you. The way you smiled at him."

I tried to pull away, but his grip tightened—not enough to hurt, but enough to keep me where I was. "Tag, let go."

"You can't." His other hand found my waist, and he pressed me against the cold stone wall, trapping me in the alcove. "Not with him."

"Please—"

"You're mine." His face was close enough to feel his hot breath against my skin. "You've always been mine."

The words I'd longed to hear before we left Dunravin were unwanted now.

"I know I said we couldn't." His fingers splayed on my hip. "I know I told you we didn't have a future. But you can't just…not Vanguard."

He leaned in to kiss me, and I so wanted to close that last inch between us and pretend he hadn't shattered me into pieces I was still trying to gather up.

But I couldn't do that to myself again.

I shoved against his chest, creating space between us. He stumbled back a step.

"Tag, you've had too much to drink."

"I'm not drunk."

"You are." My voice cracked despite my best efforts to keep it steady. "You said everything ended when we left Dunravin. Those were your words."

"I was wrong—"

"You were clear." Tears threatened, but I refused to let them fall.

"Leila—"

"I'm going to bed." I ducked under his arm, putting the width of the alcove between us before he could reach for me again. "We'll talk tomorrow. When you're sober."

"Wait—"

"No. Not like this. Not when you're inebriated and saying things you'll regret the moment the sun comes up."

His face crumpled, and in the dim light filtering through from the main hall, I could see past the Earl of Glenshadow, past the deadly operative, straight through to the boy who'd watched his parents destroy each other and vowed never to repeat their mistakes.

But I couldn't save him from himself, not when he wouldn't even try to save us.

"Good night, Tag."

I left him standing in the shadows and made myself walk back through the castle at a normal pace, refusing to run even though every instinct screamed at me to put distance between us. My feet carried me up the stairs and down the hallway to my room, moving on autopilot while my mind replayed every word, every touch, every moment I should have handled differently.

My hands trembled as I unlocked my door, worse as I locked it behind me once I was inside.

The tears came then—silent and hot, streaming down my face as I leaned against the door for support.

He'd said I was his. After spending three days at Dunravin, showing me what that could mean, then telling me it meant nothing.

I pressed my eyes with the heels of my palms, trying to stem the flow, trying to breathe through the ache expanding in my chest.

Tomorrow, I'd have to pretend my heart wasn't breaking. I'd have to be Nightingale the operative again.

I pushed off the door and removed the jumper I'd pulled on earlier, glancing at the locked door I guessed separated our rooms as I walked over to the bed. It was a stark reminder of the walls between us, of the locks he'd installed to keep me out and keep himself safe.

I climbed into bed and pulled the covers up, but sleep still wouldn't come. Not with the adrenaline coursing through my veins. Not with the memory of his hands on my waist and his body pressed against mine.

I gasped and sat up, clutching the covers to my chest when the connecting door opened.

Tag stood in the doorway, swaying on his feet. There was a desperate look in his eyes. Or maybe it was shame.

"Tag, what are you doing?"

"I'm sorry." He stepped farther into the room. "I just…I needed to…"

"You need to leave."

"Can we pretend?" His words slurred together. "Everything from earlier. Outside. Can we just…forget it happened?"

"No. We can't."

"Leila. I'm sorry. Christ, I'm so sorry." He took another step into the room, struggling to find the right words through the fog of alcohol. "I shouldn't have… I had no right…"

I stayed where I was, wishing this was a bad dream.

"Seeing you with him—"

"I need sleep, and so do you." I cut him off before he could finish that thought, before he could say more that we'd both regret. "Go," I said again, softer this time because my anger was draining into exhaustion. "Tag, just go."

He turned and walked back toward the door. "I'll lock this." His voice came out rough, scraping against the silence. "It won't happen again," he said moments before I heard it click from the opposite side.

Tears came again as I slid down until I was lying flat. I stared up at the ceiling, crying for what we could have been if he'd been brave enough to try. For loving someone who wouldn't let himself love me back. For three years of waiting and three nights of believing. I cried until I had nothing left, until my eyes were swollen and my throat was raw. Until exhaustion finally dragged me under into restless, dream-filled sleep.

The headache I woke with the next morning had nothing to do with alcohol.

I'd managed maybe two hours of sleep and spent the rest staring at the ceiling or jerking awake from dreams where Tag was in bed beside me. My eyes felt gritty and swollen, and no amount of cold water splashed on my face could hide the evidence of my tears.

I dressed in black cargo pants and a fitted long-sleeve shirt, and pulled my hair back into a tight bun that would stay out of my way underground. I glanced in the mirror and saw a woman who was exhausted, hollowed out, and barely holding herself together.

When I arrived downstairs, Archon was already in the library, with his head bent over his tablet. He looked up when I entered, and his eyes scrunched. No doubt he noticed the exhaustion I couldn't hide, if not the pain.

"Good morning," he said, watching as I crossed the room.

"Morning," I responded as I chose coffee over tea and added more sugar than I normally would.

Tag appeared in the doorway moments later, and the sight of him sent an unwelcome jolt through my chest. He looked about as good as I felt—shadows under his eyes, jaw tight, moving like someone nursing a spectacular hangover. Our gazes met for half a second before we both looked away.

"Right." Tag's voice was rough as he made a cup of tea with unsteady hands. "Let's go over the plan for today."

I sat down next to Archon.

"We'll start from the east," Tag said, tracing a route with his finger. "Split up to cover more ground. The three of us searching separately will be more efficient than trying to move as a group."

Archon nodded, making notes. "Contact checks every fifteen minutes?"

"Every ten," I suggested. "The stone will interfere with signals in some sections. We need to know right away if someone loses their connection to the comms."

Tag's jaw tightened, but he didn't look at me. "Agreed. Ten-minute intervals."

Helicopter rotors cut through the morning quiet, growing louder as the aircraft approached. We turned toward the windows, watching as it descended toward the lawn.

"Who in the hell is that?" Tag asked, pushing his chair from the table.

"I've just received a message from Typhon," Archon said, studying his mobile. "He's ordered a reassignment. I'm to head north with Prima while Vanguard takes my place here."

Through the windows, I watched Vanguard emerge, ducking under the rotors as he jogged toward the castle. He was dressed for fieldwork—cargo pants, boots, and a jacket that probably concealed at least two weapons.

Douglas, whom I hadn't seen since Tag introduced him when we first arrived, opened the front door.

"Morning, everyone. Hope I'm not too late for breakfast," Vanguard said in his usual friendly tone.

"Why wasn't I given prior notice of this change?" Tag snapped.

Vanguard's eyes darted to Archon's, then back to Tag. "I cannot say, sir."

Tag stalked from the room, mobile in hand. What did he plan to do? Challenge the decision? In my opinion, it was the right one. Not that Vanguard was here necessarily, but that it would be better if Archon led the op near Dunravin.

"Good to be working together again, Nightingale," Vanguard said once Tag was out of the room.

"Welcome to the team," I said, wondering if I should follow Tag. But what would I say? If I defended Typhon's decision, he'd likely think it was because I *wanted* Vanguard here.

"I should be on my way," said Archon, looking at me, perhaps for guidance about whether or not to wait for Tag to return. When I didn't say anything, he gathered his things and walked out.

"I already read through the files on the flight over," Vanguard said, tapping his tablet when Tag returned, scowling worse than when he'd left. "I'm up to speed."

"Great," I said when Tag didn't appear to have heard him.

The next thirty minutes passed in a blur of final preparations. Vanguard gravitated toward me, asking questions about what we'd found during our previous searches. His attention was flattering, his interest genuine, and every moment of conversation between us hurt because Tag was across the room, pretending not to watch.

We loaded our gear into packs—torches, rope, chalk for marking passages, radios, water, emergency rations in case we got turned around underground. The physical tasks kept my hands busy and gave me something to focus on besides the man who was so often the center of my attention.

"Ready?" Tag asked when we'd finished, addressing us without glancing in our direction.

I shouldered my pack, feeling the weight settle against my back. "Ready."

Vanguard did the same.

"This way," Tag said, leading us out of the castle and across the grounds.

The morning air was cold enough to see our breath, and the sky was heavy with clouds.

We followed Tag to a stone outbuilding with walls covered in ivy that had been recently cleared away, that appeared to have once been a stable or storage shed.

He pulled the heavy wooden door open, revealing stone steps descending into darkness. He clicked his torch on, and its beam cut through the shadows, illuminating rough-hewn walls.

"Comms check," he said in a clipped voice. "Nightingale?"

"Check."

"Vanguard?"

"Check."

Tag nodded once, then started down the steps.

I took one last look at the sky before descending below Glenshadow. One last breath of cold morning air before entering the labyrinth where I'd be trapped underground with Tag and the man he thought I wanted instead.

The stone steps curved downward, and the light from above faded behind us.

The temperature dropped as we descended, and the air grew damp and heavy with the smell of earth and old stone.

At the bottom of the steps, the passageway split into four directions like spokes on a wheel. Tag pulled out one of the maps, though we all knew it wouldn't help much.

"We split up here. Nightingale, you take north. Vanguard, east. I'll cover west and south. Mark your path with chalk every twenty meters, and check in every ten minutes. If you find anything—recent activity, hidden openings, anything unusual—call it in right away."

"What if we hit a dead end?" Vanguard asked, adjusting the strap on his pack.

"Mark it and backtrack. Try the next branch." Tag's gaze swept over us, avoiding lingering on me. "Given the complexity of what we might discover, we could be down here for hours, so pace yourselves. Don't go farther than two hundred meters without reporting in."

I pulled out my chalk and checked my torch battery one more time.

"Remain alert," Tag added. "There's a chance we aren't the only ones down here."

The thought should have unsettled me more than it did, but right now, the prospect of encountering hostiles felt less dangerous than spending another moment standing where I was pretending I was fine.

"Move out," Tag ordered.

I headed north as instructed. Light bounced off walls that narrowed and widened unpredictably. The ceiling dropped low enough in places that I had to duck, and water seeped through the stone, leaving mineral deposits in a line to the floor.

The silence was absolute except for my footsteps and breathing. No wind, no distant sounds from above, just the heavy quiet of earth and stone pressing in from all sides. However, for the first time since last night, I could breathe without feeling like my chest was caught in a vise.

Down here, I didn't have to keep up the pretense of Tag not mattering to me.

I marked my path with chalk—a simple X every twenty meters. The route branched twice, and I chose the left fork both times, following the slight downward slope that suggested the direction I followed might connect to the lower levels near the loch.

My radio crackled. "Comms check. Nightingale?"

"Copy. Heading north-northwest, approximately sixty meters in. Two branches, no signs of recent activity."

"Copy that. Vanguard?"

"East corridor, eighty meters. Found some old smugglers' marks on the walls, but nothing present-day."

"Copy. Next check in ten. Out."

The radio went silent again, and I continued deeper into the darkness. The route opened into a wider chamber, maybe four meters across, with three new branches. I swept my light across the space, looking for any indication of which way to go.

That's when I saw it—a scuff mark in the dust on the floor. Recent, at least from this century, judging by the sharp edges where someone's boot had disturbed centuries of settled grime. I knelt down, examining the mark more closely. The tread was modern, the kind you'd see on combat boots, not the smooth soles of hiking boots or casual footwear.

My pulse kicked up. Someone had been down here, and not long ago.

I was reaching for my radio when light spilled into the chamber from the eastern branch.

"Nightingale?" Vanguard's voice echoed off the stone. "That you?"

"Here." I stood as he emerged, his beam sweeping across the space before landing on me. "I found something. A boot print in the dust. Recent."

He crossed to where I was standing, and bent to examine the mark. He straightened, following the direction the print was heading. "Looks like they went that way."

He pointed to the narrowest of the three options. I marked the chamber with chalk and the boot print's location, taking a photo with my mobile.

"Should we follow it?" he asked, already moving toward the opening.

"We should call it in first." I reached for my radio, but before I could key it, Tag's voice came through.

"Status check. Anyone have anything?"

"Nightingale here. I found signs of recent activity. A boot print."

"Copy that. I've got a lock on your position, and I'm on my way."

"We could—" Vanguard began, but I shook my head.

"We'll hold our position until Tag arrives."

Vanguard nodded, though I could see the eagerness in his expression—the same look every operative got when they found something that might turn into a lead.

The wait felt eternal, though it was probably only five minutes before Tag's beam cut through the darkness. He emerged into the chamber, his gaze going first to the boot print, then to me and Vanguard standing too close together in the confined space.

His jaw tightened. "Good catch," he muttered before squatting near the print. When he stood, his eyes finally met mine. "This way," he said, motioning in the same direction Vanguard had a few minutes ago.

The walls pressed closer the farther we went, forcing us into single file. Behind me, I could hear Vanguard's steady breathing.

Tag's light caught another scuff mark, then another before the passage curved sharply left. There, it dropped down a series of rough-cut steps. The air grew colder still.

We continued down until we emerged into a cavern that opened up before us like a cathedral carved from living rock. Natural limestone stretched overhead, and stalactites hung from a high ceiling that disappeared into the shadows.

And on the far side, barely visible in the reach of our lights, was a door.

It appeared modern, steel-reinforced, and completely out of place in this ancient space.

Someone had been down here for more than a walk-through, and they'd gone to hide whatever was behind the door.

12

Tag

Vanguard had the lock picked and open in under two minutes.

The heavy steel door swung inward with a hydraulic hiss that echoed through the cavern, revealing the darkness beyond. I raised my torch to illuminate what lay inside.

"Christ," he muttered beside me.

The space was modern, climate-controlled, and maintained—everything the ancient cavern surrounding it was not. Metal shelving units lined the walls in industrial rows, all of them empty. The air inside held that particular sterile quality of a space kept at a specific temperature and humidity, the kind of environment required for sensitive equipment or electronics.

I stepped inside, my boots echoing on the concrete floor. Nightingale followed, her torch sweeping methodically across every surface while Vanguard remained at the entrance, keeping watch.

The shelves bore signs of occupation. Not decades or even years ago. This had been in use far more recently than that.

"Tag," Nightingale said, her voice tight with controlled urgency. "Look at this."

She stood near the center of the space, her light focused on the floor. When I reached her, the chalk marks were impossible to miss.

Someone had created a grid across the concrete, outlining where the crates had been positioned. The marks were faint but visible, laid out with exacting care—whoever had measured and marked these positions knew exactly what they were doing and where every piece of cargo should sit for maximum space efficiency.

"They were storing equipment here," I muttered.

Nightingale was already moving, photographing everything with her mobile. She worked methodically, capturing every angle and every detail.

The walls drew my attention next. The scratches on them weren't random, and the lack of dust on the shelves' otherwise dirty surfaces confirmed the deliberate placement of crates of similar sizes.

"This indicates recent activity," Vanguard commented from the doorway.

"You're right." Nightingale crouched near one of the chalk marks, angling her mobile to capture it. "These marks are fresh. No foot traffic has disturbed them, no air movement has worn them down."

What we'd discovered settled over me like a weight. This wasn't some abandoned Cold War bunker or forgotten storage facility. This was a present-day operation being conducted beneath my own estate, using infrastructure I didn't know existed. That I'd been walking above it for months, completely unaware, jarred me.

The far wall held the kind of industrial-grade equipment used for sensitive cargo. Power cables ran along the ceiling to outlets that were clearly modern installations, not part of the original construction. Whoever had outfitted this space had gone to considerable expense, and more importantly, they'd done it without anyone noticing.

"They'll come back," Nightingale said quietly, appearing at my shoulder. "Whatever was stored here, they moved it elsewhere. But they left the infrastructure intact. Which means—"

"They plan to use it again."

Our eyes met in the torchlight. For a moment, the barriers between us dropped and I saw the same fear I felt—that we were always one step behind, that whoever was orchestrating this had been planning for years while we scrambled to catch up, that people would die because we couldn't move fast enough.

Then she turned away, returning to her documentation, and the walls went back up.

The climate-control units still ran, pumping cold air into an empty room. The electricity required to run this setup wasn't insignificant. Whoever had installed it must have tapped into the castle's power supply before it reached the meters, making the drain invisible to anyone reviewing the estate's utility usage. Smart. Deliberate. The work of people who knew how to stay hidden.

We spent another twenty minutes examining every corner of the space. Vanguard checked the perimeter, looking for any other exits or hidden compartments, but the chamber appeared to be exactly what it seemed—a storage facility, emptied out, waiting to be filled again.

When Nightingale finally pronounced the documentation complete, we stood in the center of the empty chamber—three operatives surrounded by the ghost of whatever had been stored here.

"Ready?" I asked.

Nightingale nodded, shouldering her pack while Vanguard moved to the door, preparing to lead us aboveground.

One last glance around the space made me wonder how many other estates had similar facilities hidden in their foundations? How long had this network been operating? And most importantly—who was running it all?

"Tag?" Nightingale's voice pulled me from my thoughts. She stood at the door, waiting, her expression unreadable in the torchlight.

"Coming," I said, forcing myself to move.

We filed out of the chamber. Behind us, the steel door sealed shut with another hydraulic hiss, hiding its secrets once more.

But we'd found them. Whoever had been using this space would soon discover they were no longer working in the shadows.

The ascent took longer than the descent. The hours spent underground had drained us, each step upward feeling heavier than the last. Nightingale's breathing remained even ahead of me, her torch beam cutting through the darkness with unwavering focus.

My mind raced through what we'd found. The climate-controlled chamber. The chalk grid. The evidence of use within the last few weeks. Labyrinth wasn't just continuing—it was thriving, using my own estate as part of their distribution network.

We emerged into the undercroft an hour later. The late-afternoon sun filtered through the high windows, making me blink after the darkness below. The shift from the underground chill to the castle's warmth made my skin prickle.

Douglas appeared at the top of the stairs, his expression sharpening when he saw our faces.

"Find anything?"

"Get Mrs. Murray to prepare food," I said, my voice rough from hours of breathing stale air. "We need to brief Typhon within the hour."

Douglas nodded and disappeared toward the kitchen.

"We'll take a short break, during which time I'll request a conference."

"Thirty minutes?" Nightingale asked, already moving toward the doorway, with Vanguard close on her heels.

"Affirmative. We'll meet in the study."

She nodded and left.

I gave her enough time to retreat upstairs, then went to my suite to shower, hoping it would help clear my head if not my thoughts. I stood under the hot water longer than necessary, washing away the underground grime while my mind churned through what we'd discovered. Someone had been in the tunnels recently, which meant they might come back.

Once I returned downstairs, I rang Typhon. He answered on the second ring.

"Obsidian."

"Requesting a full-team conference within the hour. We found active operations beneath Glenshadow. There's evidence of use within the last few weeks."

"I'll contact the other teams. We'll convene in thirty minutes."

"Copy that," I said, ending the call when Nightingale walked in. Her hair was still damp, pulled back in a sleek knot that emphasized her neck. She'd changed into dark trousers and a fitted burgundy jumper like she often wore.

I looked away before she caught me staring.

"Coffee?" I gestured to the pot Mrs. Murray had brought in, remembering it was what she chose yesterday.

"Please."

I poured a cup, added sugar, and handed it across the desk. Our fingers didn't touch, though I was acutely aware of how close they came.

"I've confirmed a team videoconference," I said.

"I overheard," she said. "In the meantime, I'll cross-reference what we found with the intelligence from Syria."

Neither of us spoke for several minutes. The silence between us wasn't comfortable, but it was bearable—two operatives preparing for a briefing, nothing more.

Except it was so much more than that, and we both knew it.

Her teeth caught her lower lip as she concentrated, and the furrow between her brows deepened as she worked. She looked up, and this time, she caught me staring.

"What?" she asked.

"Nothing." I cleared my throat. "Just…you're good at this. Your job. Exceptionally so."

Her expression flickered—surprise, perhaps at the compliment—but it was gone as quickly as it had come.

"You made sure I would be."

"Nightingale, Leila—"

"The files are ready." She angled the laptop so I could see the screen. "We should review the presentation order before the others join."

The shutters came down, sealing her away from me again.

I stood beside her, both of us looking at the screen rather than each other, and began planning how to present what we'd found.

The videoconference went live at sixteen hundred hours. My large monitor divided into multiple feeds, showing Con and Lex in Edinburgh, Ash and Sullivan at the borders, Archon and Prima somewhere in the Northern Highlands, and Gus and Renegade calling in from what looked like a hotel room. Typhon and Viper occupied their own frames, likely both from London.

"Right then," Typhon said, his voice cutting through the ambient noise from multiple locations. "Obsidian, you called this meeting. What did you find?"

I pulled up the first image on the screen—the steel door in the cavern beneath Glenshadow.

"We discovered modern infrastructure and signs of recent activity," I began, cycling through the photos we'd taken.

"Were they moving AIWS components?" Typhon asked.

Nightingale leaned into frame. "Unknown. The space was empty when we found it. However, the setup suggests they stored sensitive equipment or electronics."

Viper's eyes sharpened. "How long has this been in use?"

"Impossible to say with certainty."

"Understood," said Typhon. "Moving on, then. Infidel, Edinburgh status?"

Con's feed expanded. "We've confirmed that James Dalgleish is the owner of the Imperial Gallery, where Lex and I noted suspicious activity during the Orlov investigation. Now, we've been able to document specifics. He's been hosting private viewings over the past seventy-two hours. High-value transactions, but the buyers aren't your typical art collectors."

Lex appeared beside him, pulling up data. "Eastern European, Middle Eastern, Asian interests—same profiles we observed during our initial surveillance. We've been able to access transaction detail as well. The amounts are substantial—six and seven figures. As Con said, the suspects are more likely arms dealers rather than art patrons."

"The Imperial Club is also back on our radar," Con added. "The private members' club where we intercepted conversations about Orlov's consortium. Dalgleish, who is a member, has been meeting with Russian interests—likely the same individuals we heard discussing 'the package from St. Petersburg' and integration timelines."

"So the gallery and club are directly connected?" I asked.

"Yes. Dalgleish uses the gallery for transactions and the club for negotiations. Classic operational separation—one location for money, another for business discussions."

"The same shell company structure we tracked to Nova Perspectives during the Orlov investigation remains active," Lex continued.

Nightingale leaned forward. "Nova Perspectives was connected to Orlov's consortium?"

"Affirmative," Con replied. "Which means whoever's running Labyrinth now was part of Orlov's operation then. The network didn't collapse after the explosion at the Inverness facility."

"Is Dalgleish your primary suspect for running the Edinburgh operation?" Viper asked.

"Based on the transaction volume and the buyer profiles, yes. But he's not working alone. This is too sophisticated for a single person."

Typhon's gaze shifted. "Archon, Prima. Northern Highlands report."

Archon's feed came forward. The nondescript background could have been anywhere in the Highlands. "We've been investigating the area north of Inverness as assigned. Thermal imaging has detected some anomalies."

"Specify," said Typhon.

"Heat signatures in areas that should be cold. We're still gathering data. Nothing conclusive yet."

The vagueness was deliberate, and from Typhon's slight nod, he understood why. Whatever they'd found near Renegade's family estate wasn't something to discuss on an open channel with this many people listening.

"Savior, borders' status?"

Ash's window expanded so Sullivan was visible beside him. "We've identified a shipping broker, Ian MacKenzie, who operates out of Berwick-upon-Tweed. His container routing shows irregularities that match Tower-Meridian's signature—the same patterns previously documented."

Sullivan pulled up shipping manifests on the screen. "There are weight discrepancies and suspicious routes through European ports. The cargo documentation lists electronics and industrial equipment, but the routing doesn't make sense for legitimate trade. Rotterdam to Hamburg to Gdansk. Each transfer creates documentation gaps. And the weight discrepancies average fifteen to twenty percent per container—always explained as 'packaging materials' or 'shipping damage.'"

"He's moving cargo he doesn't want inspected," Ash added. "And he's meeting with Eastern European contacts Thursday—we've got surveillance scheduled at the King's Arms pub in Berwick."

"MacKenzie runs a small operation on paper," Sullivan continued. "Five employees, twelve years in business, but his container volume has tripled in the past six months. He's not the buyer or the seller—he's the middleman moving components from point A to point B."

"Does he connect to Dalgleish?" Viper asked.

Sullivan glanced at Ash. "We're cross-referencing now. The timing of MacKenzie's shipments corresponds with peaks in Dalgleish's gallery transactions. If one is handling money and the other cargo…"

"They're coordinating," I said.

Typhon's gaze shifted again. "Orion, Renegade. Can you confirm that connection?"

Gus's window came forward. "We can. Dalgleish and MacKenzie are directly connected. Money flows between them through the same Cyprus and Malta shell accounts. The amounts are substantial—we're talking millions over the past six months. You'd think they'd wise up and create new in- and outflows, but that they haven't certainly works to our benefit."

"They're operating in tandem," Renegade added. "Dalgleish handles the money; MacKenzie handles the shipping. But there's a third party funding the entire operation. We're tracking back to the source, but while I agree with Gus' assessment, whoever is at the top knew how to hide their trail."

"How well hidden is it?" Typhon asked.

"Very. Multiple layers, different jurisdictions, accounts that don't connect directly. We'll find it, but it's going to take time."

Typhon leaned against his chair, processing. "So we have three distinct pieces of the puzzle—underground storage facilities, art gallery money laundering in Edinburgh, and shipping logistics in the Borders. All connected, all active right now. The question that remains is who's running it. Dalgleish and MacKenzie are assets, but they're not the mastermind. Someone with considerable means is funding this entire thing."

"We need to find Janus," Nightingale said quietly.

"We need to get close enough to both Dalgleish and MacKenzie to figure out who they're reporting to," said Viper.

"Agreed, but we do it carefully. If Janus realizes we're onto them, they'll shut it down and disappear.

We need to track back to the source before we make any moves," Typhon cautioned. "Infidel, maintain Edinburgh surveillance. Don't approach Dalgleish yet. Just watch and document. Savior, same with MacKenzie. We need to know their routines, their contacts, and their schedules before we move."

"And Glenshadow?" I asked.

"Maintain security on all entrances. If they come back to use that storage facility, I want to know immediately."

The strategy made sense, even though every instinct screamed at me to shut it down now. But Typhon was right—we needed to follow the trail back to its source, and that meant watching and waiting while Labyrinth continued under our noses.

"One more thing." Lex's voice cut through the discussion. "The buyer profiles from Dalgleish's gallery—we're running them through intelligence databases. If any of them have connections to state actors or known arms dealers, we'll identify them."

"Someone is managing all of this. We find that person, we find Janus," Typhon said before ending the meeting.

I closed my laptop once everyone had signed off and Vanguard excused himself. "Well, that was illuminating."

Nightingale stared at the now-blank screen. "They're close. Dalgleish, MacKenzie—they're close to something big. I can feel it."

The way all the pieces were aligning—the money and the logistics and the storage facilities—this wasn't the remnants of Fallon Wallace's group limping along. This was larger, better organized, and far more dangerous.

"I should check in with Douglas. Make sure the estate is properly secured."

"Tag," she started, then stopped.

I waited, hoping she'd continue, hoping she'd say something that would bridge the chasm between us.

But she just shook her head and stood. "I should review the files again. Cross-reference with what Con and Lex found."

"Right."

She gathered her things and headed for the door, then paused with her hand on the frame. "We're going to stop them. Whatever Labyrinth is planning, whoever Janus is—we're going to stop them."

"I know."

She left, and I sat wondering how much longer we could keep working together like this—close enough to touch, but too broken to reach each other.

I was about to head outside for a walk when Vanguard appeared in the doorway.

"Got a minute?" he asked.

"What is it?"

He glanced down the corridor where Nightingale had disappeared, then stepped fully into the room and closed the door behind him. "We need to clear the air."

"About?"

"I would think that would be obvious." He crossed to stand on the other side of my desk, meeting my eyes directly. "I want you to know that when Nightingale and I were in Syria, she let me know loud and clear that she wasn't interested. When I asked if there was someone else, she said there was."

I steeled my expression, even as my chest tightened. "Your point?"

"While she didn't say it specifically, I got the impression it was someone she was in love with."

I held Vanguard's gaze, refusing to give anything away.

"For what it's worth, if she was in love with me, I'd move heaven and earth to have her in my life."

He walked out before I could respond, closing the door quietly behind him.

I remained where I was, his words echoing in my head. *Move heaven and earth to have her in my life.* I wished I could. But the vow I'd made when my father died still held me like iron, and I didn't know how to break free.

Twenty-two hundred hours found me still at my desk, surrounded by evidence, trying to make sense of what we'd found beneath Glenshadow. How many other facilities were hidden down there? How many times had whoever was running Labyrinth walked beneath my feet or Ash's or Con's while we remained completely oblivious?

The whiskey bottle sat within reach, but I refrained. I'd learned that lesson already.

A few minutes after midnight, my mobile rang with a call from Gus.

"Tell me you found something," I said in lieu of a greeting.

"Every transaction funnels through Luxembourg before dispersing. I'm working on penetrating the shell structure, but this one isn't as easy to hack into."

"How long do you estimate it will take?"

"Days, maybe a week. These accounts have layers upon layers." He paused. "I'll send updates as I find them."

The call ended, leaving me alone once again. I stood, needing air, movement, a change of scenery before I went mad staring at the same documents, hoping they'd reveal secrets they didn't contain.

The library lights were on when I passed, warm against the darkness of the corridor. Through the partially open door, I could see Nightingale bent over the large table, maps spread in front of her, cross-referencing them with what looked like architectural surveys.

I should have kept walking and left her to work in peace.

Instead, I detoured to the kitchen, poured two cups of coffee, including one for me, from the pot Mrs. Murray had left warming, and returned to the library.

Nightingale was focused on tracing a line between two points with her finger and didn't look up when I entered.

"Thought you might need this," I said, setting a cup beside her.

She raised her head, and surprise flickered across her face. "Thank you."

I took the chair beside her rather than across the table, close enough to see what she was working on, but not so close I'd be tempted to touch her. "What have you found?" I asked.

"The tunnels near the storage chamber branch in three directions. One goes toward the loch, one deeper into the grounds, and one that appears to head northeast."

"Toward Blackmoor," I said, recognizing the direction.

"Exactly." She pulled another document—an architectural survey from the 1800s—closer. "According to this, the monasteries in this region were all connected by underground passages. The monks used them to travel between religious houses without being seen."

"The Jacobites expanded them later." When my hand brushed hers as we reached for the same document, we both froze.

Her eyes met mine, and for a heartbeat, the carefully maintained distance between us evaporated. I could see the way her breath caught when our skin touched.

"Sorry," she said, pulling her hand away.

"No, I—" I stopped, the words dying in my throat because, what could I say? That every moment near her was torture and relief in equal measure? That Vanguard's words kept echoing in my head—*move heaven and earth*—and I didn't know how to be that brave?

I cleared my throat. "The historical records are in the archive room. I can pull one of the monastery documents if you think they'd help."

"That would be useful. If we can chart the full extent of the original passages, we might be able to predict where else they've built facilities."

I stood, grateful for the excuse to move, to put space between us before I reached for her again.

Twenty minutes later, I returned with additional leather-bound volumes. Like the others, their pages were yellowed with age, but they were remarkably well-preserved otherwise. We spread them across the table, beside the modern layouts, comparing centuries-old survey notes with current layouts.

"Here," Nightingale said, pointing to a notation in Latin. "This mentions a convergence point—where multiple passages meet. It's marked as being beneath what used to be the chapel."

"The east wing," I said.

The work took on its own rhythm after that—she'd mark a location, and I'd find the corresponding reference in the historical records. I'd point out a connection based on my knowledge of Glenshadow, and she'd cross-reference it in the opposite direction. We moved around each other with the kind of synchronization I'd longed for, getting lost in the work rather than focusing on our mutual discomfort.

When the clock chimed zero two hundred, Nightingale rubbed her eyes. "I should get some sleep. Long day ahead."

"Leila—" How many times had I said her name, then stopped myself from saying more like I had now? Countless.

Her eyes bored into mine. "Yes?"

The words were right there. *I'm sorry. I was wrong. I don't know how to do this, but I want to try.* But my throat closed around them, and all that came out was: "Sleep well."

My chest ached when her brief smile disappeared.

"You too," she said so quietly I barely heard her before the sound of her footsteps faded down the corridor.

I waited, then took the back staircase up to the second level, rather than the main one that would lead me past her door, where the temptation to know would be too great. With each step I took, I hated my cowardice as much as I hated the fear that kept me silent.

13

Nightingale

The encrypted message came at zero four hundred, jolting me from my restless sleep.

I reached for the tablet on my nightstand, blinking against the blue glow in the darkness of my room at Glenshadow. The screen showed a single notification—priority intelligence, Kestrel's signature encryption.

My pulse quickened before I'd even opened it.

PRIORITY: TIME-SENSITIVE OPPORTUNITY

EVENT: Private charity gala

LOCATION: Brodick Castle, Isle of Arran

DATE: This evening, 2000 hours

HOST: James Dalgleish

ATTENDEES: High-value targets confirmed. Guest list includes Ian MacKenzie and international arms dealers Vadim Karpov, Hassan Al-Rashid, and Chen Wei.

ASSESSMENT: Optimal window. Dalgleish's network exposed, vulnerable. Primary targets in one location. Recommend immediate action.

NOTE: CRITICAL TIMELINE - Guest list locks at 1200 hours. After that, infiltration impossible. You have until then to decide.

This was it. The opportunity we needed. Several of our targets would be gathered in one place, at a charity gala I could infiltrate as a guest.

From Damascus to London—every lead had brought me here. To the people responsible for my brother's death.

If I brought this to Tag, he'd shut it down immediately. He'd insist on going himself, even though he'd be recognized instantly in those circles—the Earl of Glenshadow, who'd moved through aristocratic events his entire life. Or he'd refuse the op entirely.

The promise he'd made to Idris would ensure that.

I was perfect for this assignment. Unknown in aristocratic circles, trained for infiltration, fluent in the social languages required to move through a charity gala undetected. I could get close to Dalgleish and MacKenzie and their buyers, and maybe even gather what we needed to dismantle their entire operation.

Tag wouldn't be able to do the same. Nor could Con or Ash.

But me? I was nobody to these people.

The mission had to come first. Even if it meant going around Tag. Even if he never forgave me for this.

I committed every detail Kestrel sent to memory, then stood, moving to the wardrobe to pull out clothes.

Dawn wasn't here yet, but it was coming fast, and I had work to do before the rest of the household woke up. But first, I needed to make contact with Typhon and Viper. Without their support, there'd be no way for me to pull this off.

The sun was barely breaking through the tall windows of the library at zero five thirty, the time Viper had confirmed we could meet. I positioned myself at the far end of the room, away from the door, with my laptop open on the desk so the camera angle only showed my face and the bookshelves behind me.

The secure connection took thirty seconds to establish, and when the screen divided into two feeds, Typhon appeared on the left and Viper on the right.

"Nightingale," Typhon said. "This better be good."

"I have time-sensitive intelligence that requires immediate authorization."

"Let's hear it."

"There's a charity gala this evening at Brodick Castle on the Isle of Arran. James Dalgleish is hosting."

That got their attention.

Viper leaned forward. "Dalgleish?"

"Yes. My source confirms high-value attendees, including MacKenzie as well as known arms dealers."

"What's Obsidian's assessment?" Typhon asked.

My stomach tightened. "He's unaware of the intel."

Viper's brow shot up. "Explain."

I chose my words carefully. "If Tag learns about this beforehand, he'll stop me from going. He'll either refuse to authorize it entirely or insist on going himself."

"But he'd be recognized," Typhon said under his breath.

"So would Con and Ash. Every sensitive conversation would shut down the moment they walked through the door." I leaned forward. "I'm lesser known, and with the right hair and makeup, I'm better suited. I can infiltrate as a guest, get close to the targets, and gather as much intel as possible. This is exactly what I was trained for."

"Your tactical assessment about this opportunity is sound," Typhon said. "And you're right that MacTaggert would be compromised in that environment."

Relief flooded through me.

"However…" Viper's voice was sharp when she cut in. "We don't authorize operations behind a handler's back. That's not how MI6 functions."

My stomach dropped. "But—"

"Unit 23 will authorize the mission," barked Typhon. "But MacTaggert will be informed. As soon as the op is secure."

"But—" I repeated.

"You heard me."

The words came out before I'd fully thought them through. "Then I quit. Effective immediately."

Silence crashed across the connection, and Viper's expression sharpened. "Leila—"

"I have to do this. With or without support from SIS."

"This is enough to refuse you and inform MacTaggert," she spat back at me.

My eyes met Typhon's. "If I don't do this, Idris' death will be in vain. And, Typhon, I will never forgive you." I turned to Viper. "Or you." I took a deep breath. "You both know I have the means to ghost. I've done it before, and I can do it again. I may lose this chance, but there will be another. I'll make sure of it."

Neither spoke for several seconds. Finally, Viper did. "Very well. I'll serve as your handler again, but only for this mission. You'll have full op authority, but you'll report directly to me."

"No. She'll report to me, given my unit is authorizing as well as funding this," Typhon clapped back. "But I have another caveat. Vanguard goes with you. If necessary, I can pull him from the Glenshadow assignment."

"I accept those terms."

"I'll arrange your cover identities, wardrobe, and logistics." Viper's eyes were steady on mine as she spoke, as though she hadn't heard a word Typhon said. "The fallout from this is yours to handle. When Tag finds out—and he will find out—you'll deal with the consequences."

"I understand, and I will. So, who do I report to?"

When they both answered, "Me," Typhon smirked and shook his head. "Both of us. But never again. Got it?"

"Roger that."

The feeds disconnected, leaving me staring at a blank screen in the growing dawn light.

My hands trembled as I closed the laptop. The weight of what I'd just done set in. Once again, I was ruining any chance I'd have to be with the man I loved. But hadn't he already made that decision for me?

I stood and returned to my room to prepare for a day of careful omissions and half-truths with the one person I'd never wanted to deceive.

Tag found me in the library midmorning, looking every bit like a man who'd slept well and had no inkling of the subterfuge taking place at his estate.

"Making progress?" he asked, nodding toward the plethora of notes on the table.

"If Labyrinth has facilities at Glenshadow, they likely have them elsewhere too."

He moved to stand beside me, close enough that my chest tightened with what I was about to do.

"We'll need to check Blackmoor and Ashcroft systematically. Con and Ash should search their estates when they return," he suggested.

"That makes sense."

We worked in silence for the next hour, in what should have been an easy collaboration. Except it wasn't. Every word I spoke was a careful navigation around the truth.

When my tablet buzzed with an encrypted message from Viper at eleven hundred thirty, I angled it away from Tag as I opened it.

Cover established. Helena Moore, art collector, recently divorced. Background verifiable through multiple sources. Wardrobe and documentation being delivered to hotel in Brodick. Vanguard briefed. Extraction protocols in place. Deploy 1645 hours.

I deleted it quickly, but not before Tag noticed.

"Everything all right?"

"Viper was confirming some logistics." Not a lie, but not the whole truth either.

His brow furrowed. "For?"

This was it. The moment when I crossed the line from omission to active deception.

"Vanguard and I are heading out this afternoon to conduct additional reconnaissance on the estate connections and thermal signatures."

The lie came out smoothly. I'd practiced it during the hours since my call with Typhon and Viper.

"This is the first I've heard of it."

His mobile rang before I could respond, and when he glanced at the screen, his expression hardened. "What do you know? Viper's calling now."

"MacTaggert." His eyes remained riveted to mine when he answered.

I couldn't hear her side of the conversation, but I watched his jaw tighten as he listened to whatever she was saying.

"I wasn't consulted about this reassignment." His tone of voice was low, the way it got when he was fighting to maintain control. "She's my operative."

He paused while Viper responded to his challenge.

"Thermal signatures requiring the chief of MI6's personal oversight?" Skepticism dripped from every word he spoke. "For routine reconnaissance?"

Another pause followed while his free hand clenched into a fist at his side.

"And this couldn't wait for proper briefing because...?"

Whatever Viper said in response made his expression darken further.

"Understood."

He ended the call with barely controlled anger, then stood perfectly still for several seconds while he visibly worked to regain his composure.

"Viper says the intelligence is time-sensitive and that source verification required her direct involvement."

His tone made it clear he didn't believe a word of what he'd just been told. "She's concerned about the London surveillance incident and wants extra security protocols in place."

The lies I'd set in motion tasted bitter in my mouth. "Tag—"

"Why didn't she brief me directly rather than wait until you're about to walk out the door?"

"I can't speak for her."

"Right." His gaze lingered like he was searching for answers. "Be careful," he finally said.

"I will."

The words sickened me, but what choice did I have? I had to do this. For Idris.

At thirteen hundred, Vanguard and I met at a small pub in Tarbert and sat in a corner booth where no one would overhear as he walked me through the op's parameters.

"Viper's thorough," he commented, sliding documentation across the table. "I'm Richard Sutherland, financial consultant. We met at a gallery opening six months ago and started dating a few weeks later."

"It's solid," I said after scanning the cover story.

"Extraction plans are better." He pulled up a diagram of Arran. "Three routes off the island if things go sideways. Helicopter on standby in Brodick, boat access at two harbors, car positioned for mainland escape."

"Signals?" I asked.

"Standard. Weather comment for immediate extraction. Adjust your earring if you need backup but can stay in play. Finish your drink to exit a conversation naturally."

We spent the next hour running scenarios—potential complications, backup plans, how to handle security, and where the safe points were inside Brodick Castle.

When we finished an hour later, it was time for me to return to Glenshadow to gather my things.

"Just so you know…" Vanguard's eyes met mine. "I'll have your back at that gala."

"You know I'll have yours."

"And MacTaggert's going to hate us both when he finds out."

His words hit hard. He was right. Tag would never forgive me.

I put off speaking to Tag again until it was fifteen minutes before Vanguard would arrive. I found him in his study and poked my head in.

"Leila? What can I do for you?"

My stomach clenched.

"I wanted you to know I was leaving."

His eyes were hooded. "Be careful."

"Always."

Vehicle lights appeared outside the window.

"I'll walk you out."

"That isn't necessary—"

He was out from behind his desk and over to me before I could finish my sentence. "I insist."

The walk to the SUV was torture. With every step I took, I thought about aborting the op and telling him the truth. But I couldn't. I had to finish this. And while that might not happen tonight, whatever did take place would put us one step closer.

We were within a few paces of where Vanguard had parked when Tag stopped and turned to face me.

"Nightingale—" His hand lifted, reaching toward my face, and for a heartbeat, I thought he might actually touch me. Break through the distance he'd maintained since Dunravin. But then his fingers curled into a fist and dropped back to his side.

"I should go." I cut him off before he could finish, before the words between us made leaving impossible. "I don't want to keep Vanguard waiting."

I picked up my bag and walked away, glancing over my shoulder to take one last look—that's all I'd allow myself.

"You okay?" Vanguard asked when he drove out of Glenshadow's main gate.

"I will be. Once this is over."

Ninety minutes later, Brodick Castle rose against the twilight sky—six centuries of stone and battlements looking down on expensive vehicles owned by people with the kind of wealth that could move weapons across continents.

After checking into the hotel, we went to our separate rooms, where we'd transform ourselves into our alter egos for the night.

"We have about two hours before we need to leave for the castle," Vanguard said when we reached my door at eighteen hundred.

"I'll be ready." I went inside and stood in the silence.

I started with the practical stuff, putting a small pistol in a thigh holster that would remain hidden beneath my gown. Then I put on the earring that was really a comms device.

Next, I began the transformation, first styling my hair in loose waves. Then I applied heavier makeup than I typically wore. The emerald silk dress Viper had chosen slid over my skin, and the accompanying jewelry glittered at my throat and wrists. I studied myself in the mirror, barely recognizing the woman I saw.

There was a knock at the door, and when I opened it, Vanguard stood in the corridor, transformed into Richard Sutherland in an impeccably tailored tux.

"Last chance to back out."

I picked up my clutch and checked that everything I needed was inside. "I'm not backing out. Let's finish this."

He offered his arm, and I took it, stepping fully into the Helena Moore persona. I closed my eyes for a moment, sending a silent message to Idris, but instead of my brother, Tag's face appeared. *Forgive me*, I said silently.

We walked toward the castle's entrance, where Dalgleish and his network waited and where I hoped to gather intelligence that would make this deception worth it.

A man in evening wear examined our invitations. "Ms. Moore, Mr. Sutherland," he said before returning them with a courteous nod. "Welcome. The gala is through the next set of doors."

The grand hall soared above us with rows of crystal chandeliers that cast warm light over guests whose jewelry was as real as mine was fake. Waiters circulated with champagne, and a string quartet played in the corner.

I scanned the room, picking up on conversations.

"Champagne?" Vanguard settled his hand on my lower back and offered me a glass.

"Thank you, darling," I said, sounding far more like Helena Moore than myself.

We moved through the crowd, making small talk, laughing at appropriate moments, and playing our roles while searching for our targets.

I spotted Dalgleish near the center of the hall. His silver hair was perfectly coiffed, and he was standing with

Ian MacKenzie. Surrounding them were well-dressed men whose faces rarely appeared in photographs.

"There," I murmured to Vanguard.

"I see them."

We circulated closer, stopping first to speak with a banker from London, then an American tech investor, followed by a French diplomat's wife.

Gradually, we worked closer to Dalgleish's circle.

A woman examining a medieval manuscript gave me the opening I needed.

"The pieces here are remarkable," I said. "Though I confess I'm more interested in modern acquisitions."

"Are you a collector?" she asked in a heavy German accent.

"In a modest way. Contemporary European artists, primarily." I offered my hand. "I'm Helena Moore."

"You should speak with James—our host. He has excellent connections."

Exactly what I'd hoped she'd suggest.

When she caught his attention with a subtle gesture, he excused himself and joined us.

"I don't believe we've met," he said, offering his hand.

The woman made introductions, then drifted away.

His eyes sharpened as we fell into a conversation about art that seemed more like a negotiation as he measured my knowledge and whether I was serious. All the while, MacKenzie studied me in a way that rattled me.

"I'm hosting a viewing next week at my gallery in Edinburgh," Dalgleish said after several minutes. "Selected pieces, eager buyers only. Perhaps you'd be interested?"

"I'd be delighted."

He gestured to the men beside him. "Allow me to introduce my colleagues. Ian MacKenzie, Vadim Karpov, Hassan Al-Rashid, and Chen Wei."

Vanguard positioned himself nearby—close enough to intervene, but far enough to maintain pretense— while I shook each of their hands.

The plan was working—until I saw someone that stunned me speechless. Across the Great Hall, talking with two men in formal wear, stood Mr. MacLeod, the estate manager from Dunravin. What was he doing here?

"Ms. Moore?" Dalgleish's voice summoned. "Are you quite all right?"

I forced a pleasant expression. "Forgive me. I thought I saw someone I knew, but I was mistaken."

But when MacLeod's gaze swept the room and landed on me, the flicker of recognition in his eyes confirmed it.

No amount of makeup, fancy hairstyles, or elegant gowns could hide my real identity. He knew exactly who I was, and I'd just blown my cover.

14

Tag

After Nightingale left, everything felt wrong, though I couldn't say why.

I called Typhon within minutes of the vehicle disappearing down the drive. "The Viper assignment. I want details."

"MacTaggert." His tone gave nothing away. "She's handling op specifics on this one."

"Since when does she handle routine reconnaissance personally?"

"Given what happened in London, extra precautions seemed warranted," he responded.

"That's not an answer."

"It's the only one I'm authorized to give." There was something he wasn't saying. I was certain of it. Was it an apology? A warning? "Trust that Nightingale's safety is the priority."

"If her safety was the priority, she'd be here. Not running thermal reconnaissance with Vanguard under mysterious circumstances that no one will properly explain."

"Tag—" He paused as if he wasn't sure what to say next. "If anything develops, you'll be informed immediately."

The careful phrasing set alarms off in my head. "If anything develops." Not "when they report in."

My next call was to Viper, but her assistant claimed she was in a classified briefing. For two hours. Then another meeting. Then unavailable.

While Douglas and I spent the rest of the afternoon documenting what we'd found in the tunnels—critical intelligence requiring immediate analysis that should have consumed my attention—I was distracted, checking my mobile every few minutes.

Thus far, I hadn't received a message from Nightingale. That wasn't unusual when operatives were in the field. Silence was standard when working reconnaissance. But everything felt different this time. Heavy. Like the pressure drop before a storm.

"Sir?" Douglas's voice jarred me from my reverie. "The measurements for the eastern passage?"

I forced my attention back to our work, tracing the route we'd marked earlier. "Approximately forty meters from the junction to the first branch point. Stone construction consistent with eighteenth-century work."

Douglas glanced up at me, frowning. "Everything all right, sir?"

"Fine." The word came out sharper than intended.

His expression said he didn't believe me, but he had the good sense not to press.

I checked my mobile again ten minutes later, then thirty, muttering under my breath each time there were no alerts. Not that I cared about anyone other than Nightingale.

She was with Vanguard—I told myself. Following up on thermal signatures in the Highlands, checking potential estate connections. She said they'd be gone two days, possibly three. It was routine intelligence gathering that shouldn't require constant contact. So why did her absence feel like a wound?

Douglas gathered his notes, sensing I was done being useful. "I'll compile these for your review, sir."

After I thanked him, he closed the door behind him, leaving me surrounded by the evidence of a conspiracy that threatened national security, and all I could think about was the way Nightingale had looked at me before she left—as though she was saying goodbye.

Not "see you in a few days." Not the casual departure of an operative heading out for routine work. *Goodbye.*

I'd dismissed it at the time, too focused on maintaining distance between us, on not reaching for her the way every instinct screamed at me to do.

But the look haunted me now. The sadness in her hazel eyes, the set of her shoulders, the way she'd paused before walking away. What had I missed?

As evening settled over Glenshadow. I walked the corridors, checking systems that didn't need to be. At one point, I stood outside her room. The door was closed, of course, no light shining beneath it. God, how I wished she were behind it.

No matter how many times I told myself she was fine, the hollowed-out feeling in my chest said otherwise.

I poured whiskey I didn't drink, stared at maps I'd grown sick of looking at, and waited for a message that didn't come.

I marked the passage of time by each chime of the clock on the mantel.

At twenty-one thirty, my mobile rang with a call from Typhon. My heart hammered as I lunged to answer it. "MacTaggert."

"Tag, listen." My breath caught when I heard an urgency to his words. "Nightingale and Vanguard infiltrated a gala Dalgleish hosted at Brodick Castle on the Isle of Arran—"

"Arran? She's supposed to be—"

"I know what we told you. Viper and I...bent the truth. Nightingale came to us with time-sensitive intelligence. She knew you'd stop her from acting on it, and frankly, she was right. We made a judgment call."

Every muscle in my body went rigid. "You lied to me."

"We compartmentalized, and right now, that distinction doesn't matter because her emergency beacon just activated. Her cover is blown, and MI6 backup support lost contact with her as well as Vanguard four minutes ago. I'm mobilizing now."

My stomach dropped. "I'm already moving," I said, grabbing my vest from the cabinet.

"MacTaggert, she came to me because—"

"We'll discuss how this happened after I fucking get her out," I barked, ending the call. I pulled up emergency contacts on my phone and sent a group message. *Code Icarus. Brodick Castle. Isle of Arran. Rally point follows.* I hit send, broadcasting the emergency to every member of the team.

Responses came within seconds:

Con: *Inbound. Arran ETA 25 minutes.*

Ash: *On our way. 22 minutes.*

Archon: *Approaching. Holding for orders.*

Renegade: *En route with Prima.*

"Sir?" Douglas appeared in the doorway, gear already on, reading the situation with the instinct of a man who'd spent twenty years in special forces. "The helicopter will be here in four minutes."

It wasn't fucking fast enough.

But I nodded and finished my weapons check. My Glock was in my shoulder holster, my backup piece was secured at my ankle, and my knife at my belt. The pocket in my vest held extra magazines and comms equipment. I had everything I'd need to breach a medieval castle and extract an agent from hostile custody.

Not an agent—Nightingale. Leila. The woman I loved, who'd lied to my face earlier today.

She'd looked me in the eye and told me she was doing reconnaissance work. She even let me walk her out to the vehicle where Vanguard waited. Every word she spoke had been a calculated deception. Every moment planned to get around me.

Because she'd known I'd stop her. Known I'd refuse the op. Known I'd insist on going myself, or lock her down at Glenshadow—anything to keep her safe.

And she'd been right.

The thought sliced deep. She'd gone to Typhon and Viper because I couldn't be trusted to put the mission first where she was concerned. Because of my promise to Idris, my fear of losing her, my inability to separate professional duty from personal terror—all of it made me a liability.

So she'd cut me out entirely.

The sound of the helicopter grew louder as it approached. I grabbed my go-bag and headed for the door.

Douglas fell into step beside me. "Do you want me to come with you, sir?"

"No. Stay here. Secure the estate."

"Roger that."

I emerged onto the east lawn as the blade touched down, whipping the Highland grass into a frenzy. I ran toward it, bent low, and climbed in. "Go. Push it as hard as you can," I shouted.

The pilot nodded once. "Aye, sir. Arran in twenty minutes."

As we lifted off, Glenshadow was swallowed by darkness.

I turned up the comms and patched into the response Typhon was coordinating. Multiple voices overlapped—team leaders checking in, Viper coordinating with MI6, Typhon directing the assault.

"Infidel here." Con's voice was steady and calm. "Tag, if you're listening, Lex is with me."

Good. I registered it distantly. Lex—we'd need her if this went sideways.

"Savior and Orion inbound." Ash's voice carried the same controlled readiness. Knowing him and Gus the way I did, the two of them were probably pushing their helicopter to its limits.

"Renegade, Prima, and I are approaching the castle perimeter." Archon's transmission crackled with interference.

"All teams, converge on Brodick Castle," Viper commanded. "Stealth approach. The gala is still in progress, which means we have civilian presence to consider. We need this contained."

"Archon, your priority is finding Vanguard," said Typhon. "His signal went dark, but he's still on premises."

"Roger that."

Through all the chatter, my mind got stuck on one thing. This was my fault. If I hadn't pushed her away at Dunravin. If I hadn't thrown what we had back in her face. If I hadn't been so terrified of becoming my parents that I'd destroyed us both, then she wouldn't have gone behind my back. Wouldn't have taken this risk.

Except that was bullshit, and I knew it.

This wasn't about me. It had never been about me.

This was about justice. About stopping the people who'd killed Idris. She would have gone after Dalgleish whether I'd broken her heart or not.

I closed my eyes. *Keep her alive. Let me get there in time.* The prayer surprised me—it had been eighteen years since my father's funeral, when I stopped believing in a higher power. Now, though, I meant every word.

"Sir, Arran's ahead. Five minutes to landing."

I opened my eyes and looked to the island that rose as a dark mass against darker water. The castle was visible on the eastern shore.

The comms crackled again. "Archon here. We're in. Moving through east wing."

"Infidel, your ETA?" Typhon's voice demanded.

"Four minutes."

"Savior here. Six minutes out."

Everyone was converging like we always had. A team. Except this time one of our own—my own—was in peril.

The chopper descended toward the eastern lawn, away from the main entrance. I unbuckled before we'd fully landed, the rotors still spinning as my feet hit the ground.

Another blade touched down thirty meters away. Con emerged first with Lex right behind him, both in tactical gear with weapons ready. Con's eyes found mine across the darkness. No words were needed.

A third chopper landed, and Ash and Gus jumped out.

We moved in, using the gardens for cover, and the comms crackled again.

"We found Vanguard." Archon's voice was tight with urgency. "North wing, service corridor. He's unconscious but breathing. Head wound. Getting him out now."

"Wait. He's trying to speak," said Prima. "I think he's saying 'north tower.'"

North tower. The beacon signal confirmed it.

"All teams, check in." Typhon's voice.

One by one, they did as he commanded.

"Prima and I are extracting Vanguard," Archon reported last. "Then we'll join you."

We moved through the gardens in formation, avoiding the terraces where gala guests still gathered—smoking, laughing, drinking, completely oblivious to the armed operatives passing twenty meters away. We slipped through a service entrance, into stone corridors lit by medieval torches and modern fixtures.

The four of us in front moved in synchronized silence, weapons ready, every sense alert. We'd done this a thousand times before—Syria, Prague, Beirut, a dozen other cities where violence waited in the dark.

We reached the base of the north tower and went inside. A stone staircase spiraled upward, narrow and steep. Perfectly defensible, terrible for assault. Medieval architects knew their business.

I looked at Con, Ash, and Gus. "We get her out," I said. "Whatever it takes."

Con's eyes met mine. "Whatever it takes."

Ash and Gus nodded, and we started up the stairs, counting steps. When we hit thirty, I could hear voices, muffled but distinct. Multiple people. Male. Scottish accents.

As we neared the top, we came to a heavy wooden door with light showing beneath. The voices coming from behind it were clearer now, though still indistinct.

I signaled—*breach on three*.

The team got in position, and my hand grasped the heavy metal latch as Typhon's voice came through the comms, quiet and clear. "Obsidian has command. All teams: Nightfall. Execute."

15

Nightingale

The champagne glass nearly slipped from my fingers. My grip tightened before the crystal could shatter against the marble, but my pulse hammered loud enough that I wondered if Dalgleish could hear it.

Mr. MacLeod stood under an archway that led to a room adjacent to the one we were in. Instead of the work clothes I'd seen him in at Dunravin, tonight he wore a perfectly tailored dinner jacket and had the bearing of someone who belonged with people who bought weapons disguised as art.

I forced myself to maintain a pleasant expression while my mind raced. MacLeod being here confirmed Dunravin was compromised. The tunnels we'd found, the warnings he'd given us—all of it took on new meaning.

After asking if I was all right, Dalgleish continued talking—something about a Flemish painting he'd recently acquired. I responded appropriately while tracking the estate manager's movement through the crowd. He stopped to speak with Vadim Karpov, the Russian arms dealer whose specialty was former Soviet weapons. Their conversation was brief but familiar. MacLeod moved on to Hassan Al-Rashid, the Syrian broker known for moving chemical weapons precursors through legitimate pharmaceutical companies. Chen Wei had drifted toward another group near the bar, and I caught sight of Ian MacKenzie near the terrace doors, watching everything with the alertness of someone expecting trouble.

MacLeod's exchange with each man followed the same pattern—a handshake, a few words, a subtle nod. He was confirming something with each of them.

"The piece is from a private collection in Prague," Dalgleish continued, oblivious to my divided attention. "The previous owner was quite reluctant to sell until I made him an offer he couldn't refuse."

"How persuasive of you," I murmured, watching MacLeod signal to someone near the service corridor.

"Would you excuse us for a moment?" Vanguard's voice was smooth as his hand settled on the small of my back. His fingers tapped twice, paused, then tapped three more times—our signal asking what was wrong.

"Please don't let me keep you," Dalgleish said, stepping away.

Vanguard leaned in close enough that his breath warmed my ear. "Problem?"

"The estate manager from Dunravin is here. One o'clock. Closely cropped gray beard."

His eyes cut across the room, found the target, and returned to mine with the same question I was asking myself.

"Coincidence?" His tone said he didn't believe in those any more than I did.

"Not sure yet." I touched his arm, feigning affection while my fingers found his pulse point—rapid but con-trolled. "It is disconcerting."

"We should consider extraction," he murmured against my hair.

"Not yet. I need to know what Dalgleish knows."

Our host returned a few moments later, his silver hair catching the chandelier's light. He wore the same smile, but something in his eyes had shifted. The warmth had vanished, leaving behind the look of a man recalculating the odds. MacLeod must have signaled him somehow.

"Ms. Moore, it occurred to me that you might be interested in seeing a few of the pieces I've installed in the castle's private gallery. They are available only to the most discreet collectors."

The invitation sounded casual, but his body language screamed trap. His weight had shifted to the balls of his feet, ready to move. His right hand stayed close to his jacket, where a shoulder holster would sit. Behind him, I counted three men in servers' uniforms who'd stopped circulating with their trays.

Vanguard's hand tightened on my elbow. He felt the shift in the room's temperature as I had.

"What a kind offer." I forced warmth into my voice while my mind ran through the escape routes. The main entrance was forty feet away through a crowd. The terrace doors were closer, but MacKenzie still lurked there. The service corridor might work if we moved fast enough. "Perhaps another time."

"I insist." Dalgleish gestured toward the archway where I'd first spotted MacLeod, then grasped my arm with more force than necessary. "This way."

Vanguard's hand fell away from my elbow as Dalgleish yanked me forward. Behind us, I heard a brief scuffle—a grunt, the meaty sound of impact, then something heavy hitting the floor. They'd separated us, and from what I'd heard, not gently. I caught a glimpse of one of the fake servers wiping blood from his knuckles as he rushed by us alone. Vanguard's blood, most likely.

I tracked the footfalls coming from behind us. The gait was wrong for servers—too balanced, too ready. These were soldiers.

Dalgleish stopped at a heavy wooden door located in an area where the corridor grew darker as it narrowed. Medieval torches provided the only light, their flames casting shadows on the stone walls. When he turned to face me, his expression switched to sinister.

"Ms. Moore." He practically seethed. "Or should I say, Agent Nassar?"

"You're mistaken."

One set of footsteps behind me stopped.

"Come now, lass." MacLeod's words were heavy, weighted with reluctance. "We both know that's not true."

Our eyes met for a moment, and I saw regret there, but also determination. Whatever had brought him here, he'd made his choice long ago.

Ian MacKenzie emerged from the shadows behind MacLeod, his expression cold and calculating. "We're wasting time. An extraction team could arrive at any time."

"They won't." Dalgleish's confidence was absolute.

I calculated exits, distances, and odds. One corridor stretched behind me with MacKenzie and MacLeod blocking it. Dalgleish stood in front, and an unknown number of other adversaries lurked nearby. I had no good options for escape. My weapon remained strapped to my thigh, but even if I could reach it, I'd be dead before I could raise it to shoot.

"Where is Mr. Sutherland?" I asked.

"Your partner is being dealt with," said Dalgleish, confirming my suspicion. "Mr. Sutherland—or should I say Morse?—won't be joining us. He's currently unconscious in a storeroom, though whether he stays that way depends entirely on your cooperation."

"What did you do to him?"

"Nothing permanent yet." Dalgleish's cold expression never changed. "But head wounds can be so unpredictable. Without proper medical attention in the next hour or so…"

He let the threat hang between us.

My hand moved toward my clutch. If I could just trigger the beacon—

"Dinna do that, lass." MacLeod's voice carried a warning.

But I was already moving. I made the choice in a heartbeat, finding the small bump through the silk and leather. When I pressed hard with my fingertip, the device gave the slightest vibration, and I knew the signal had been sent. As I triggered it, I let my clutch fall to the floor with the clasp open so our backup team from MI6 would at least know the location I'd sent the alert from.

"What did you just do?" Dalgleish lunged forward, but MacLeod was faster.

I saw the syringe too late. The sharp sting in my neck was followed by frost spreading from the injection site. My legs buckled as the drug hit my system—something fast-acting, probably midazolam or another benzodiazepine.

As my vision fractured, I managed to pull off my earring and let it fall. It hit the stone with a tiny sound that seemed to echo in my fading consciousness.

I tried to fight, but my body had stopped obeying as I was lifted and carried.

Tag, I'm sorry. For lying. For going around you. Please find me.

Darkness pulled me under—absolute and final—and everything went black.

My consciousness returned in layers of pain. My skull pounded while my mouth stayed dry, and my vision swam when I tried to open my eyes. The smell of mildew told me I was still at Brodick, that they hadn't moved me far.

Stone walls rose on all sides when I forced my eyes to focus, and narrow windows showed darkness outside. Zip ties cut into my wrists behind me, while my ankles were bound to the legs of a heavy wooden chair. It was made of solid oak, probably weighing more than I did, and bolted to the floor—someone had prepared this space for holding prisoners.

My neck ached where the needle had gone in, and bruises were forming on my arms where they'd grabbed me. But nothing was broken and nothing was bleeding, which meant they wanted me alive, at least for the time being.

A table against the far wall held a computer terminal. Its screen showed what looked like deployment codes and geographical coordinates—Scotland, Northern England, Wales with red marks indicating major cities like London, Edinburgh, Glasgow, Manchester, and Cardiff as target zones.

I pulled against the restraints, testing their strength. The zip ties were law enforcement grade, designed to hold up to two hundred and fifty pounds of pressure. I could break them given time and leverage, but doing so would make noise and alert my captors. The chair's construction prevented me from getting the angle I'd need anyway. Waiting and assessing what I was dealing with before making my move would be better.

Voices filtered through a door that muffled the conversation. Multiple men spoke with accents heavy enough to place them as local, but the words themselves stayed just out of reach. I did recognize one voice—MacLeod's. He sounded agitated, like he was arguing with someone.

"—I told you this was moving too fast—" His voice rose enough to carry.

"You're in no position to question the timeline." Another Scottish voice, cultured and icy.

Footsteps sounded outside the door, and a key turned in the lock.

My spine went rigid, I pulled my shoulders back, and lifted my chin. Every line of my body declared that I was still dangerous, still a threat, still someone who would fight given half a chance.

The door swung open.

MacLeod entered first. His shoulders were hunched forward, and his hands stayed loose at his sides. Then, another man entered. Everything else faded to background noise when he stopped inside.

He was older and wore an expensive suit that was probably custom tailored. Authority lived in every line of his body, in the way he moved, in the way MacKenzie, MacLeod, and Dalgleish deferred to him without a word. This man was in charge, giving the orders they followed.

His face was familiar. I'd seen him before, or perhaps his photo, but the drugs still clouding my system made it hard to place him. The shape of his features, the way he carried himself, the cultured affectation that emerged when he spoke—all made my skin prickle.

He stepped forward and studied me as he was examining a specimen. "Agent Nassar. Welcome." He clasped his hands behind his back and moved closer. "I apologize for the restraints. They are a necessary precaution. I'm sure you understand."

He was pleasant and almost warm, as if we were meeting for tea instead of in a castle where I sat bound to a chair.

I kept my voice level. "I understand you're making a mistake."

His brow rose. "Oh? How so?"

"Every MI6 and Unit 23 operative in Scotland will converge on this location at any moment. You should run while you can."

"Your emergency beacon." He gestured to the clutch on the table near the computer I'd noticed. "Yes, we're aware you activated it. In fact, we're counting on it. Your handler will be here soon enough, I imagine."

The way he said "handler" made my blood chill.

"Who are you?"

His expression shifted to satisfaction. "You may call me Janus."

The air left my lungs. The mastermind stood in front of me, close enough that I could see the lines around eyes that suggested sixty-some years of life. This was the man who'd orchestrated everything—Fallon Wallace, the weapons, all of it.

"I've been looking forward to meeting you." He circled my chair slowly, like a predator sizing up prey. "Your work in Damascus was impressive. You were thorough when you connected Fallon Wallace to Chimera. Quite clever." He paused behind me, where

I couldn't see him. "Though you did discover rather more than I'd have preferred."

My mind worked through the details even as the drug still made my thoughts sluggish. Why did he seem so bloody familiar?

"You're wondering who I am." He stopped in front of me and read me as easily as I'd read countless targets. "Whether you've seen me before." His expression turned knowing. "You'll figure it out soon enough. Your rescuer certainly will. If he gets this far." He paused, savoring the moment. "He knows me quite well. In fact, since he was eight years old."

Tag knew him? Since he was eight—that meant this was someone from his childhood, someone who'd been part of his life for decades.

"What do you want?"

Being direct was my only option since there was no point in games now.

"The answer is quite simple. I want to change the world."

He paced like a lecturer in a classroom, warming to his subject. "AIWS isn't just a weapon, Agent Nassar. It represents the great equalizer. For centuries, power has belonged to those born to it. Titles. Land. Inheritance passed down through bloodlines as if accident of birth made someone worthy." Bitterness crept into the cultured tone. "But AIWS gives power to those who earn it, who build it, who control it."

"You mean those who steal it," I countered.

"Steal?" He laughed. "From whom? From governments that use technology to oppress? From aristocrats who hoard wealth while others starve? No, my dear. We're not thieves. We're revolutionaries."

His words belied old wounds and old anger at a system that had wronged him. He'd dressed revenge up as revolution, convincing himself that destruction was justice.

Understanding dawned about MacLeod's involvement. He'd warned us away from certain areas beneath Renegade's family's estate not because they were compromised, but because they were part of Labyrinth's network. MacLeod had been working for them all along, using his position to provide access to multiple estates.

The door opened behind him.

"Ah. Perfect timing."

Someone else entered, but I couldn't see past Janus. The footsteps that followed were hesitant, uneven.

He stepped aside, and I recognized the woman who stood in the doorway as Dr. Evelyn McLaren.

My breath caught. She was alive but looked nothing like the woman from the files I'd studied or the poised academic who'd created MI6's AI Ethics division. Her clothes hung loose on a frame that had lost too much weight too quickly, and the shadows under her eyes looked like bruises. Her hair hung unwashed around a face that had aged beyond her years. Her left hand trembled with what looked like neurological damage.

"Doctor, I believe you know of Agent Nassar." Satisfaction colored Janus' tone. "Her work has been… inconvenient for us."

The woman's lips pressed together, and her chin quivered. She forced herself to meet my eyes. When she did, I saw her trying to communicate something— her gaze flicked to the computer, then back to me, then to the computer again.

"We've never met." The words came out hoarse, as if she hadn't used her voice in days or had screamed herself raw. "But I know of her work."

I understood then. She was the Architect, but not by choice. She was a prisoner being forced to work on AIWS, to rebuild what she'd tried to destroy at the facility in Inverness.

Janus' hand settled on her shoulder—possessive, controlling, the casual touch of someone who owned another person. She went rigid, and her breathing quickened, but she didn't pull away.

"Dr. McLaren has been invaluable to our project." She recoiled with each word. "She understands our work better than anyone. Neural interface technology. EMP integration. Recursive learning algorithms." His fingers tightened on her shoulder, and she winced. "All her expertise, finally being used as it should."

She stared at me with dilated pupils and a clenched jaw, then mouthed a single word when Janus looked away. "Codes."

"Together, we're going to change everything." He released her shoulder. "AIWS will launch within days, and those with whom I share it will become the world's new superpowers. Russia, China, certain Middle Eastern interests—they've all paid handsomely for the privilege."

He turned back to McLaren. "Isn't that right, Doctor?"

"Yes." Her voice was barely audible.

But she found my eyes again in that moment, and I saw past the terror to the determination. The woman she'd been still existed somewhere beneath the broken shell he'd created. Her fingers moved slightly at her side—she was writing something against her leg. I recognized the first three, then figured out the rest. D-A-M-A-S-C-U-S.

"Now then, Agent Nassar." His attention returned to me. "We'll wait for your handler to arrive. I do hope he hurries." His expression made me shudder. "I'm quite looking forward to our reunion. It's been far too long since I've seen young Niall. I have so much to tell him about his family's role in all of this."

Tag knew this man, had history with him, and was coming here not just to rescue me but to walk into a trap. I was the bait, and I couldn't warn him.

16

Tag

My Glock was raised and tracking as splinters of ancient oak settled across the floor. Con swept left while Ash went right, and Gus covered our rear with the synchronization that came from carrying out countless missions together.

The tower room stretched before us—circular walls, narrow windows showing the night sky, medieval architecture that had witnessed centuries of violence. But nothing like this.

Then we froze.

Every single one of us stopped dead in the doorway because of who stood in the center of the room—Ambrose Ashcroft. Next to him sat Nightingale, who was bound to a chair, with cold steel aimed at her head.

Brose. Ash's uncle, the man who'd wandered through our childhood summers with his stories about art and his absent-minded charm, the doddering fool we'd tolerated at family gatherings, who'd asked me countless times about purchasing pieces from Glenshadow's east gallery, now appeared calm and amused with a weapon in one hand and his mobile in the other with his thumb pressed firmly against the device's screen.

I surveyed the scene in a heartbeat. Nightingale's wrists were zip-tied to the seat's arms, and her ankles were bound to the legs. Bruises marked her throat and arms. Blood had dried at the corner of her mouth. But her eyes tracked everything.

"What the fuck…" Con's sharp intake of breath cut through the silence.

Beside me, Ash staggered as if he'd taken a blow to the chest. "Brose?"

The man barely looked at him. The absent-minded uncle had vanished. This was someone else entirely—someone who'd hidden behind eccentricity for decades.

"Evelyn?" Lex's voice was just above a whisper when she came around us and saw her mentor alive, standing near a computer terminal.

McLaren didn't acknowledge her. She kept typing, her fingers moving across the keyboard with determined speed. Whatever she was doing, she wasn't going to stop.

Renegade's voice carried a betrayal sharp enough to cut. *"MacLeod?"*

His family's estate manager stood near the door with his head down, refusing to meet anyone's eyes. The man who'd welcomed us to Dunravin, whose wife had fed us, who'd warned us about dangerous passages, was part of this. The hits kept coming.

There were two other men in the room—Dalgleish, who'd positioned himself by the window, with his weapon drawn and tracking our entry, and Ian MacKenzie, who stood near the door, blocking the only other escape route.

"Hello, boys." Brose's tone was conversational, as if he were greeting us at the pub for drinks. "It's been quite a while since we were all together." He raised the device. "If my finger leaves this screen, AIWS will launch. So let's all remain calm."

The standoff crystallized with brutal clarity. We had the numbers—five armed operatives against four hostiles—but Ambrose controlled two things that mattered above all else—Nightingale's life and the AIWS trigger that would activate the moment we took him down.

Con's weapon tracked between Ambrose and Dalgleish, his stance perfect despite the shock of betrayal. Ash kept his aim steady despite his uncle standing before him as the enemy. Lex stood beside me with her sidearm raised as she stared at McLaren.

Silence stretched between us. Then Ash broke it with a single word that sounded ripped from his throat. "Why?"

Ambrose's expression shifted. The mask slipped, and decades of resentment crawled out from underneath—raw and venomous after a lifetime of being buried.

"Why?" His laugh was bitter. "Your father took everything from me. The title. The estate. The inheritance. George received all of it because he was born first." His words built in intensity. "Birth order gave George everything and left me the scraps."

His knuckles had gone white around the weapon's grip, but the barrel never wavered from Nightingale's temple. She sat absolutely still, reading him the way she'd been trained to read targets. His thumb remained pressed against the mobile's screen, steady despite the tremor in his voice.

"Do you know what it's like?" Ambrose continued, his voice rising. "To grow up in the same house, receive the same education, have the same blood running through your veins, but know that you'll always be less? George got Ashcroft, the London townhouse in Belgravia—seven bedrooms overlooking Hyde Park. The Scottish estates—three of them, including the grouse moors that brought in two million annually. The art collection—a Rembrandt, two Turners, a Caravaggio that museum curators begged to display. I got a trust fund that wouldn't buy a decent flat in Mayfair and the expectation that I'd be grateful for it."

He laughed again, ugly and sharp. "I was smarter than him. I understood culture in ways he never could. But none of that mattered. And then he took Alexandria." The words came out quiet, which made them worse. "The woman I loved was happy with me until my older brother decided he wanted her. We'd been together for a year, we were planning a future, and then I brought her home to meet my family. Six months later, they were married and I was invited to the wedding. I had to stand in the chapel at Ashcroft and watch him marry the only woman I'd ever loved."

Beside me, Ash stilled. He knew the story, just not the tragic ramifications of it.

"Then I met Fallon Wallace." Ambrose's expression hardened. "At an auction at Sotheby's ten years ago. She was bidding on a Caravaggio, driving the price up just to watch the aristocrats squirm. She saw me watching and approached during the champagne reception. She knew exactly who I was—the forgotten younger brother of the Duke of Ashcroft. She'd done her research."

He shifted, but the barrel didn't move from Nightingale's head. "She introduced me to others like me. Dalgleish is the Duke of Moorheath's younger brother. His sibling inherited eleven estates and an art collection worth fifty million pounds. James got a gallery startup loan and a pat on the head."

Dalgleish's expression didn't change, but his grip on his weapon tightened.

"MacKenzie—the spare heir of Stormbridge— works as a shipping broker while his older brother runs the family empire. He takes orders from men he went to school with, men who treat him like hired help because his brother holds the title."

MacKenzie's jaw clenched, but he remained silent.

"And MacLeod—forever in his brother's shadow, managing the family's estates like a servant." MacLeod flinched. "His own family's properties, and he's treated like staff." Ambrose glanced at Renegade. "And your family's as well."

"We call ourselves the Forgotten Sons," Ambrose continued with a smirk. "We met at the Imperial

Club, but it wasn't until Fallon Wallace provided the resources and connections that we understood our real purpose. She knew what it meant to be denied your birthright—she'd built an empire from nothing while watching incompetent men inherit fortunes. Together, we were going to create a new world order. One where power was earned, not inherited."

"Brose—" Con took half a step forward.

"Don't." Ambrose's thumb twitched on the mobile screen. "One more step and I release it."

He looked at each of us in turn—at Ash, the nephew who'd inherited everything when his father died; at Con and me, earls in our own right; at Gus, who'd recently discovered his own aristocratic bloodline.

"All of you were born into wealth and privilege you never had to fight for." His eyes had gone too bright. "You've never known what it's like to be overlooked, dismissed, treated as less than, despite being equal in every way that matters. AIWS is power that can't be taken away by birth order or family trees."

"This isn't you." Con kept his aim steady. "You're family."

Ambrose's sneer was ugly. "Family? None of you ever cared whether I existed. You tolerated me at gatherings, humored me, but did any of you ever really see me? I was furniture. Background noise."

"You haven't earned anything." Ash's voice broke halfway through. "You've destroyed everything. For what? For revenge? Your actions won't bring my mother back or make you the heir. Nothing will change except prove you were never worthy of any of it."

Ambrose started to respond, but movement on the laptop screen caught his eye. His head snapped toward McLaren at the terminal.

Even from where I stood, I could read the display. *Unauthorized Access. Administrative Override in Progress.*

His face went white, then red with rage.

"Step away from that terminal! Now!" he screamed.

McLaren had been working silently the entire standoff, her thin frame hunched over the keyboard. Twenty feet separated her from where Ambrose held his weapon to Nightingale's head. All focus had stayed on him, on the threat, on his mobile—and she'd used the distractions.

She didn't pause. She kept entering code with the desperation of someone who knew they had one chance.

"I rescued you!" Ambrose's voice cracked with fury. "I pulled you from the burning building when everyone else ran. I nursed you back to health, gave you purpose again."

"You imprisoned me." McLaren turned to face him, thin and exhausted but with her spine straight. "You kept me drugged for weeks until I was too weak to resist. You threatened to hurt innocent people if I didn't comply. This was supposed to prevent war, not enable terrorism."

The screen behind her continued scrolling—*Accessing Core Protocols.*

"I gave you everything!" Ambrose continued his rant. "Resources, equipment, the freedom to perfect your work!"

"You gave me chains disguised as opportunity." McLaren's voice held steady now. "I helped create AIWS to prevent nuclear war, to give governments a non-lethal option. You've perverted it into a tool for mass murder."

Ambrose was stuck. He couldn't remove the threat from Nightingale, because that was the only thing stopping us from advancing on him. That meant he couldn't stop McLaren, and he couldn't release the mobile.

"I said to stop, now!" he screamed again.

Like before, she ignored him.

I saw his intent a second too late—the slight shift in his stance, the way his arm tensed. Ambrose raised his weapon and fired. The shot cracked through the chamber. McLaren jerked forward against the keyboard, her hands clutching at the desk for support. I lunged, but Ambrose swung the barrel back to Nightingale's head, still clutching the mobile in his other hand.

"Don't move!" he shouted at us as McLaren slid from the chair, blood soaking her shirt. She reached toward Lex with trembling fingers, then shifted her gaze to Nightingale.

"Damascus…" Each word cost her. Blood frothed at her lips. "Codes…"

Her breath rattled in her chest.

"Finish it…"

Her hand dropped, and her gaze went blank, as if fixated on something none of us could see.

Lex made a sound as if she'd been gutted. She tried to move forward, but Con caught her arm even as she fought against him.

"Lex, stop." Con held her back. "You can't help her. She's gone."

She stopped struggling but couldn't look away from McLaren's body collapsed near the terminal.

The silence stretched. Then the laptop screen flashed again—*Administrative Override 47% Complete.*

"No!" Ambrose's head snapped toward the terminal, and his weapon swung away from Nightingale as he lunged for the keyboard.

I charged across the room. Twenty feet disappeared in seconds. Ambrose jerked back with his focus split between the terminal and maintaining his grip on both weapons. For a fraction of a second, his thumb lifted from the mobile screen.

The laptop blared an alert: *Countdown Initiated. Ninety Seconds to AIWS Deployment.*

"No!" Ambrose's eyes went wide as he realized what he'd done. The mobile tumbled from his hand, clattering across the floor as he twisted toward me.

The room erupted into motion. Dalgleish raised his weapon toward Con, but Ash was faster—a single shot hit him in the chest. The man's sidearm spun away as he fell backward. MacLeod moved to intercept me, but Renegade caught him, using his momentum to slam him against the wall with enough force to drive the air from his lungs. MacKenzie raised his aim toward

Con, but Lex was already moving. Her shot found its mark—shoulder, not fatal but incapacitating. When he dropped, his weapon skittered away.

Ambrose jerked the barrel toward Nightingale, but I was already there. I hit his arm as he squeezed the trigger, and the shot went wild. The bullet punched into the wall behind us, sending chips flying. We grappled for control, spinning across the floor. I locked both hands around his wrist, but he was stronger than he looked. Years of bitterness and rage fueled muscles that shouldn't have held against mine.

"You don't understand!" he snarled, spittle flying. "You've had everything handed to you!"

Con reached Nightingale, and his knife flashed as he cut through the zip ties. She stumbled up from the chair, her legs unsteady after being bound for so long. Lex pulled her back toward the wall, away from the fight.

The weapon remained trapped between us. Ambrose twisted hard, trying to angle the barrel toward me. I drove my knee into his ribs and felt something give—a crack that meant broken bones. His grip loosened for half a second, and I ripped the weapon free, sending it across the flagstones toward Gus.

Now, we faced each other with no gun between us and no leverage for either side.

He swung wildly, but I blocked it and drove my fist into his solar plexus. Air rushed out of him in a whoosh, but he came back with a punch that caught my ribs. Pain flared, but I'd taken worse.

"You don't understand!" he repeated in a ragged voice. "You never understood!"

I blocked his next swing and grabbed his arm, using his momentum to flip him. "You're right. I don't understand killing innocent people. I don't understand betraying family. I don't understand becoming a monster because you didn't get what you wanted."

Across the room, Ash moved to help Renegade secure MacLeod while Gus covered MacKenzie's fallen form and kicked his weapon away.

I spun Ambrose around and slammed him face-first into the floor. His head cracked against the flagstone with a sound like a breaking egg, and his body went limp.

Con was there at once, securing him with zip ties he'd pulled from his vest.

Red numbers pulsed on the screen. The countdown was still running as sixty seconds blazed in text.

"What did you do?" Con's knee pressed harder into Ambrose's back.

Ambrose's cackle erupted from beneath Con's weight. The sound belonged to a man who'd lost everything and decided to take the world with him.

"I held it as long as I could, but you made me drop it." Blood showed on his teeth from where his face had connected with the floor. "This is on your conscience, not mine."

Fifty seconds remained.

"Every networked system on the planet crashes." His voice rose, triumphant despite his defeat. "Hospitals go dark. Planes fall from the sky. Cars with electronic ignition stop working. Traffic systems fail. Emergency services go blind. Life support machines die." His grin sickened me. "And we're in Scotland when it goes live. We all die here. Everyone loses."

"No!" Nightingale yelled, moving toward the laptop.

Con tried to stop her, but she shook him off.

"The codes." Her voice cut through the panic. "I have the codes."

I stared at her. "What codes?"

Forty-five seconds blazed red.

"From Idris." Nightingale was already at the keyboard, with her hands hovering over the keys. "The encrypted files my brother left me. I memorized everything but didn't understand what they were until now."

The pieces fell into place—Idris's death, the investigation he'd been running, the information he'd tried to protect. "The AIWS kill codes?"

"Yes." Her fingers hit the keys.

"McLaren must have given them to him. Her last words meant something. Damascus codes. Finish it."

I moved beside her. "It's all we have."

Forty seconds remained.

Ambrose's face had gone white. "You can't. Those codes don't work. We tested them. We made sure—"

But his panic said otherwise.

Nightingale started typing, entering the first string—a long alphanumeric sequence that seemed to go on forever. The system immediately responded—*Authentication Required.*

She kept going with the second string, even longer than the first. *Secondary Authentication Required* appeared on the screen.

She entered the third code, the longest one yet—numbers, letters, symbols in a sequence that made no sense to me but clearly did to her. Forty characters. Forty-five. Forty-six.

My heart hammered against my ribs as thirty seconds remained, but Nightingale hesitated.

"Leila?"

"Forty-seven characters." Her voice wavered. "I remember forty-six. What's the last one?"

Behind us, Ambrose sneered despite Con's knee on his back. "You can't do it. You'll fail. Everyone dies because you can't remember one character."

"Close your eyes." I leaned closer, my hand on her shoulder. "You memorized it. Idris trusted you with it. The answer is in there."

She did, and her face went still. Then her lips moved, running through the sequence again.

Time slowed as each second became an eternity. Twenty seconds remained.

Her eyes snapped open. "Seven. The last character is seven."

When she entered it, the word *Processing* appeared. More authentication challenges appeared—security protocols that McLaren must have built in, layers upon layers designed to prevent exactly what Nightingale was attempting. But she kept going, entering code after code. Her fingers didn't hesitate again. They moved, driven by the confidence of someone who knew exactly what they were doing.

The countdown reached fifteen seconds.

"That's it." Her voice shook. "Final sequence."

The shortest code contained ten characters. If she was wrong, if she'd misremembered anything or gotten a single digit out of order, civilization would end in seconds.

She hit ENTER.

The air felt too thin to breathe as ten seconds appeared.

Processing remained on the display while everyone held their breath.

Ambrose sneered beneath Con's weight. "Too late. You're too late."

My hand found Nightingale's shoulder as five seconds appeared.

Four seconds.

Three seconds.

Two seconds.

Then the screen changed.

Shutdown Sequence Initiated.

Neural Interface Disabled.

EMP Components Deactivated.

All AIWS Systems Terminated.
Countdown Canceled.

The laptop went dark. The hum of active electronics faded to silence. Components that had been ready to destroy civilization powered down into harmless metal and circuit boards.

Nightingale stepped away from the terminal, her whole body shaking now that the adrenaline was crashing. She'd done it. She'd saved the world with seconds to spare.

Movement behind us came sharp and sudden.

Ambrose twisted beneath Con's restraint, his bound hands reaching for something we'd missed. His fingers found his ankle, and metal glinted in the dim light as he yanked a compact derringer from a concealed holster—he'd have two shots, enough to kill at close range if he got them both off.

"No one wins!" His voice cracked with rage and desperation. "If I can't have what I deserve, no one—"

A shot rang out. Ash's bullet struck Ambrose in the chest, and he jerked backward. The small firearm clattered from his fingers, unfired. Red darkened his expensive shirt, spreading quickly through the fabric. His eyes went wide with shock, then confusion, then nothing.

He slumped to the flagstones and went still.

Silence crashed down around us.

Ash's hand trembled, and his face drained of color as he lowered his gun with his hand. He'd just killed his uncle.

Con's hand gripped Ash's shoulder. "You did what had to be done."

Ash didn't respond. He just stared at Ambrose's body.

I caught Nightingale before her knees gave out and pulled her against my chest. She was alive. We were all alive. And AIWS was dead.

"It's over," I said into her hair. "You did it. Everything's over."

But looking around the room—at McLaren's body, at Ambrose's still form, the blood pooled around Dalgleish, at MacLeod weeping against the wall, at MacKenzie, who may or may not still be breathing—I knew it wasn't over. Not really.

The aftermath was just beginning.

17

Gunshots still echoed in my ears—sharp cracks that had ended four lives.

I couldn't look away from McLaren slumped against the terminal where she'd made her final stand, the Damascus codes, her last gift to the world. Blood had pooled beneath her, dark against the stone. Her eyes remained open, fixed on nothing, but I felt like she could still see me. Behind us, I could hear Lex crying while Con murmured something low and comforting. Ash said nothing, but his silence carried more weight than words. He stood over his uncle's body, the gun still in his hand.

"Leila." Tag's voice cut through the fog, and his hands gripped my shoulders. "We need to go."

I nodded, but my feet wouldn't move. The drugs MacLeod had injected still clouded my system.

"Now." He pulled me toward the door, with his arm around my waist, holding me upright when my legs threatened to give out.

But I couldn't leave yet. I pulled away and moved to McLaren's body, kneeling beside her despite Tag's protest. Her hand was still warm when I took it.

"Thank you," I whispered.

I closed her eyes gently, the way Idris had taught me to honor the dead. When I stood, Tag was there, ready to catch me if I fell.

We passed MacLeod on our way out. Renegade had him secured with zip ties, but the fight had gone out of him completely. I stopped in front of him. His eyes met mine—broken, desperate, seeking something I couldn't give him.

"Is your wife involved in this?"

He shook his head. "She knows nothing. I kept her out of it. My daughter too. Isla's in Norway, doing research. She has no idea what her father has done…" His voice cracked. "What will happen to them?"

"That's not for me to decide," I said, stopping myself from pitying him. He'd made his choices, and he'd pay the price.

Tag's hand found the small of my back. "We need to keep moving."

He stayed by my side as we made our way down the spiral stairs, each step jarring injuries I hadn't noticed yet. My wrists were raw from the zip ties. No doubt they bore angry red marks that would turn purple by morning. My throat ached where someone—Dalgleish most likely—had grabbed me. The injection site on my neck throbbed with each heartbeat.

Through the corridors, we passed MI6 response teams sweeping the castle. They'd arrived just minutes after we'd stopped the countdown. The gala guests were being evacuated, most of them oblivious to how close they'd come to being at ground zero for a global catastrophe.

"Agent Nassar needs medical attention," Tag barked at a passing operative.

"Medical staging area is just off the main room, sir."

Tag changed direction, guiding me through unfamiliar hallways. My vision blurred at the edges as the sedatives fought their way out of my system.

"I'm fine," I mumbled.

"You're not," Tag said, his arm tightening around me. "You were drugged, beaten, and nearly—" His jaw clenched, and he stopped himself.

The room we entered had been transformed into a field medical station. Vanguard sat on one of the antique settees, holding an ice pack to his head while a medic checked his pupils.

"Nightingale!" He started to stand but swayed.

"Sit down, Morse," the man attending him ordered.

"Is he all right?" I asked.

"Concussion, but he'll live," the man replied. "Now, let's look at you."

Tag helped me onto an examination table they'd set up. Another medic—a woman with kind eyes and steady hands—began her assessment while Tag hovered, refusing to move more than a foot away.

"Bruised ribs, two, maybe three." She pressed gently, and I hissed. "Gashes on wrists, contusions on throat, arms. What did they inject you with?"

"Midazolam, I think. Maybe something else. I was unconscious for at least thirty minutes."

She shone a light in my eyes, checking pupil response. "Any nausea? Double vision?"

"Some nausea. Vision's a bit fuzzy."

"We'll run bloods to be sure, but it looks like you're metabolizing it normally." She turned to Tag. "She needs rest, fluids, and observation for the next twelve hours. No strenuous activity."

Tag's hand found mine, and he nodded.

"Nightingale." Viper's voice came from the doorway. She entered with Typhon at her side. They must have come directly from London the moment my beacon activated.

I tried to stand, but the medic pressed me back down. "Stay put."

When Viper approached, her composure cracked momentarily, but she quickly recovered. "Your beacon activated at twenty-one forty-seven. We mobilized everything we had."

"What in the bloody hell happened?" Typhon said, his voice gentle despite the curse.

"Idris left codes for me. I didn't understand what they were until tonight." My words were vague, certainly not accurately conveying the hell we'd lived through, but each one cost me energy I no longer had.

"You saved the world," Viper said simply.

The weight of it settled on my chest. I'd been focused on the immediate threat, on Tag finding me, on stopping Ambrose. But the scale was staggering.

"The full debrief can wait," barked Typhon. "Get her out of here. We'll handle cleanup."

They left, and the medic finished her examination. "You're lucky. Nothing's broken, nothing that won't heal. But you need rest."

Tag helped me stand. In the corner, I saw our team gathering. Con had his arm around Lex; Gus stood with Renegade, both of them silent; and Ash sat alone, staring at nothing.

I pulled away from Tag and went to him. He looked up as I approached, his eyes hollow.

"I'm sorry," he said quietly.

I sat beside him and took his hand. "You saved my life. Not just mine. You've nothing to be sorry for."

"I know." His voice broke. "My father's own brother turned into someone evil and twisted. How do I explain it to the world?"

"You can't. You are not responsible for his actions or his mental state."

He squeezed my hand, then let go. "Thank you. For memorizing those sequences. For stopping it."

I wanted to say more, to ease his pain, but there were no words for this. Sometimes, people we loved became monsters. Sometimes, we had to stop them. The cost was always higher than we imagined.

Tag knelt in front of me. "The helicopter's here. Time to go."

Outside, the night air hit my lungs like ice, sharp and clean after the mustiness of the castle. The chopper waited with the rotors already spinning, and the pilot stood by the open door. His eyes widened when he saw me—the marks on my throat, the blood on my clothes that wasn't all mine, the way I was shaking.

"Get us home. To Glenshadow," Tag told him.

Glenshadow. The word felt foreign and perfect all at once.

Tag helped me into the cabin and climbed in after me. As we lifted off, I watched Brodick Castle fall away below us—that tower, that room, those bodies. Emergency vehicles covered the grounds. So many people had responded to clean up our mess, to hide what had almost happened from a world that would never know how close it had come to ending.

My body shook harder as we flew over the dark water toward the mainland. My teeth chattered despite the heated cabin.

"Shock is setting in," Tag murmured, pulling me against him.

But it was more than that. The adrenaline that had kept me functional was crashing, leaving behind the raw reality of what had happened.

"I'm sorry," I whispered against his chest.

His arms tightened. "Not necessary."

"But I lied. I went to Viper and Typhon instead of you."

He was quiet for several seconds. "I would have stopped you."

"I know."

"If you hadn't been there, if you hadn't had those codes…"

"McLaren would have found another way."

"No." His voice was firm. "She was dying. She knew she had seconds. She gave you the clue because she knew only you would understand."

The tears came then—hot and unstoppable. For Idris, who'd died protecting this information. For McLaren, who'd died activating it. For MacLeod's wife and daughter, who would wake tomorrow to find their world destroyed. Even for Ambrose, the broken man who'd let bitterness turn him into a monster.

Tag's hand moved through my tangled hair, murmuring words I couldn't make out over the helicopter's noise but understood anyway.

When we touched down on Tag's estate, Mrs. Murray stood in the doorway, waiting. She took one look at Tag and me and raced toward us.

"Oh, lass," she said, putting her arm around me. When Tag let go, her embrace was fierce and warm and everything I needed. "Thank the Lord in heaven you're all right."

When she pulled away, her eyes were wet. "I'll have a bath drawn. Food will be waiting when you're ready." She looked at Tag with an expression that held both worry and trust. "Take care of her."

"I promise I will." His words sounded like a vow.

Douglas appeared. "Sir?"

"Get in touch with Typhon. I anticipate a briefing if not tomorrow, soon." Ever efficient.

"Roger that. I'll take care of everything."

Tag grinned as he squeezed the man's shoulder. "Thank you, Douglas."

The walk to my room felt endless. Each step sent pain through my ribs. Tag remained by my side, holding as much of me as he could and ready to catch me if I stumbled. When we reached my door, he hesitated.

"The heating's acting up again. Best if you're with me."

"Your room then," I said quietly.

He let out a breath of relief, then led me to his suite.

His rooms were warmed by a fire already crackling in the hearth. The bathroom was full of steam, the claw-foot tub already filled and waiting. Mrs. Murray had anticipated everything.

I stood, staring at the water, unable to make my body move. My hands shook as I tried to reach behind me to unfasten my tattered gown.

"Let me do it." Tag's voice was soft.

He lowered the zipper and eased the fabric off my shoulders. Marks on my arms were already vivid—purple and black where they'd grabbed me. He traced one gently, his jaw tightening. "I should have been there sooner."

"You came exactly when I needed you."

He helped me out of my undergarments after removing my weapons that Ambrose and his goons had been too crazed by power to look for. Not that I would've been able to reach them.

He was careful of the injuries on my ribs, and when I was naked, he guided me into the tub. The heat sank into my bones. I closed my eyes and let myself float.

"I'll give you some—"

"Stay." The word came out as a plea.

He pulled a stool over and sat beside the tub. After a moment, his hands moved to my hair, working shampoo through the tangles. Neither of us spoke. The silence was enough—proof we were both here, both alive, both whole enough to put back together.

His fingers found a knot and worked it free gently. The simple domesticity of it—Tag washing my hair while I soaked away the nightmare—made my chest tight with emotion.

"I thought I was going to die." The words tore out of me. "When I realized who Janus was, when he said he knew you, I thought you'd walk into his trap and we'd both—"

"We didn't, and that's all that matters."

When the water cooled, Tag helped me stand and wrapped me in a heated towel before pulling me against him.

"I didn't trust you." The confession came from somewhere deep inside him, and I leaned away so I could look into his eyes. "I didn't trust that we could be different, that we wouldn't become my parents."

"We won't. Not ever." I touched his face.

His eyes closed, and he leaned into my palm.

"I thought I'd lost you." His voice cracked. "When that beacon activated, when I realized where you really were—I thought I'd lost you before I could tell you how much I love you."

The words hung between us, honest and vulnerable.

"I love you too." My voice broke. "I've loved you for so long."

His forehead dropped against mine. "How can you forgive me? For pushing you away? For making you feel like you couldn't trust me?"

I pulled him closer. "Just love me. That's all the apology I need."

"I do. God, I love you so much."

"Then show me."

He carried me to the bed even though I could walk, but I understood—he needed this, needed to care for me after hours of being unable to protect me. The sheets were cool against my heated skin, and he stood beside the bed, looking at me like I was precious, like I might shatter if he wasn't careful.

I reached for him. "Please, Tag. Be with me."

"You're sure?" His voice was rough. "After everything—"

I pulled him down, and the kiss we shared started out soft, then deepened.

"I need you," I whispered against his mouth as he settled beside me. "I need to feel alive."

Understanding crossed his face. This wasn't just about desire—though I ached for his touch—but about proving to ourselves that the worst was over.

When he entered me, it was slow and reverent, and his eyes never left mine. Every movement was gentle, conscious of my injuries but also of what we'd both nearly lost.

"I love you," he said.

"I love you."

We moved together unhurriedly, savoring each touch and kiss and breath. This was a promise being made in the language of bodies, a vow that we'd chosen each other despite everything that had tried to tear us apart.

When release came, it washed over us—profound and gentle and perfect. He pulled me against him after, holding me close as exhaustion tugged at my consciousness.

"Sleep," he murmured against my hair. "I'll be here when you wake."

His heartbeat was steady beneath my ear as darkness pulled me under—not the terrifying dark of the tower, but the peaceful dark of safety and home and love.

Tomorrow would bring debriefs, decisions, and consequences for the choices we'd all made. MacLeod would face justice while his wife and daughter faced shame. The world would keep spinning, never knowing how close it had come to stopping.

But tonight, in Tag's arms, with his breath warm against my hair and his heart beating steady beneath my palm, I was exactly where I belonged.

18

Tag

The castle was silent except for Leila's breathing beside me. I'd been awake for an hour, watching her sleep, cataloging each bruise like evidence of my failures. The purple marks on her throat formed a necklace of violence. Her wrists bore matching bracelets where the zip ties had cut deep. The medics had cleaned and bandaged the worst of it, but nothing could erase what had been done to her.

My mobile vibrated on the nightstand—Douglas with the inevitable summons. *Typhon and Viper have arrived. Library. 0900.*

I checked the time—zero eight thirty. When I shifted to check the message more carefully, she spoke without opening her eyes.

"How long have you been watching me?"

"An hour. Maybe two."

"Creepy, MacTaggert." But her hand found mine beneath the covers. "When is the inquisition?"

"Thirty minutes."

She opened her eyes. "Help me up. Everything hurts."

I did, supporting her weight as she stood. She moved like someone three times her age, each step carefully taken to minimize pain.

"Shower," she said. "Then war paint."

"War paint?"

"Makeup to cover these." She gestured at her throat. "I'd hate for your sister to see me like this. She'd probably be horrified."

"Wait, what do you mean?"

"Con made the arrangements."

I thought about how long it had been since the three of us were together. Years, it felt like.

"I can't wait to meet them." I saw something in Leila's eyes then. Regret maybe? Or was it simply the sadness that came along with missing her brother?

"They'll love you, just like Idris loved me." I winked, but her expression turned even more serious.

"He did, you know. He trusted you and wanted me to know I could too. In fact, and this is very hard for me to admit…"

"Go on."

"Initially, my brother wanted me to contact you. More, to hand off what he'd given me."

In my gut, I'd wondered if that had been the case. However, Idris should've known better. Known that she would never do that. I rubbed the ache that settled in my chest, wishing he could see the woman his sister had become—strong, fierce, stubborn, independent, and most importantly, loving.

"Tag?"

My eyes met hers. "If you'd done as he asked, I'm not sure if I could've saved the world in the same spectacular way you did."

"You're teasing—"

"Yes, but I also mean every word. You were meant to carry on your brother's work. *You.* I'm glad that I was able to be at your side for some of it, as I'm sure many others on the team are, but as you said to me more than once, you could and did handle much of it on your own."

"You're not angry?"

I smiled. "How could I be anything other than proud? And I mean that sincerely. Idris would be too."

"Thank you for saying that."

"They aren't empty words, Leila."

She nodded once. "I know they aren't."

While she showered, I stared at the breakfast tray Mrs. Murray had delivered—full Scottish breakfast, tea, toast, all of it growing cold. Morag Murray had been with my family for forty years, since before my mother left, taking care of three motherless children, one of whom grew up to be an assassin for the Crown. She'd seen us through every crisis, every injury, every loss. Now, she was seeing us through this.

Leila emerged from the bathroom twenty minutes later, dressed in dark trousers and a high-necked sweater that covered her throat. She'd applied concealer with the skill of someone who'd hidden injuries before, but I could still see the damage underneath if I looked closely. And I was looking very closely.

"Stop staring," she said, pulling her still-damp hair into a severe bun. "We need to go."

"You could stay here. Rest. I'll handle the debrief."

"Like hell." She moved past me toward the door. "I need to hear everything. Understand everything. That's how I'll process this."

The walk downstairs took longer than usual. She gripped my arm, pretending it was affection rather than necessity.

Voices carried from inside my study when we approached. I recognized Typhon's deep rumble, Viper's clipped tones, and surprisingly, my brother Cameron's laugh. The sound stopped me—when was the last time I'd heard him laugh in this house?

The room looked different with the morning light exposing every mote of dust, every crack in the ancient leather bindings. Someone had rearranged the furniture, likely Gus and Douglas, and brought in extra chairs that formed more of a circle rather than the formal arrangement we usually used. It made the medieval room feel less like a tribunal and more like what we actually were—a group of people trying to make sense of horror.

Typhon stood when we entered, as did Viper. The rest of the room went silent.

Cameron and Maggie stood too, and walked over to us.

"Thank you for being here," I said when they approached.

Maggie was the first to embrace me, then my brother did, but neither spoke.

"This is Leila," I said, as if her name alone conveyed everything she was to me.

"It's lovely to meet you both," she said, stepping forward to embrace them like they had me. I almost warned them not to hurt her, but apparently, they'd been briefed about her injuries, based on how gentle they both were.

"We've been advised that our presence will not be required during your meeting," said Cameron.

"Forbidden is more like it," Maggie muttered.

"Mrs. Murray has taken pity on us, though, and insisted she has a special treat for us in the kitchen. As though we're still children."

I chuckled. "I think she'll always see us that way."

Maggie squeezed my hand. "We're staying on here, if that's all right with you."

I turned to face her. "This is your home as much as it is mine. It always has been, and it always will be. I hope you know that."

Her eyes filled with tears. "I do, but—"

"But nothing. Stay on as long as you'd like. In fact, I'd not mind if you never left."

Both my siblings raised brows, and I chuckled again.

"Save me some of Mrs. Murray's special treat," I called out when they left.

"Not a chance, big brother," Cameron said over his shoulder.

"Shall we?" I said, pulling out a chair for Leila.

I sat beside her, took her hand in mine, and squeezed. She squeezed back as I glanced around the room at those gathered.

Con and Lex sat as close as Leila and I were, and I noticed Lex's hand gripped his with white-knuckled intensity. McLaren had been her mentor, her friend, and the woman who'd shown her how to be brilliant in a world of dangerous men. Witnessing her bravery in the face of certain death was something she'd never forget.

None of us would.

Gus sat at a table, his laptop open in front of him. My guess was he'd worked through the night, tracking money with renewed vigor, now that he had a better idea where to look.

Renegade looked haggard, worse than I'd ever seen him. Dark circles ringed his eyes, and his usual fluid grace had been replaced by the mechanical movements of someone running on autopilot. He took a seat by the window, staring out at the Highland morning as if answers might be hidden in the mist.

Archon and Prima had arrived together, then Ash entered last with Sullivan. I was glad she was here. It was her investigation into Eric Weber and Tower-Meridian that led us all to this point. If it weren't for her intransigent nature, God only knew what the Labyrinth Project would've turned into.

"Before we get started," Typhon said, "you'll want to know that Vanguard is recovering well. His injuries, the worst of which is a concussion, were serious but not life-threatening. He's at the military hospital in Glasgow and should make a full recovery within a few days."

"Thank God," Leila murmured, and I saw the guilt she'd been carrying ease.

"He sends his regards," Viper added. "And his apologies for not being here."

"Let's begin," Typhon said once everyone was settled. "The immediate threat is neutralized, but we need to understand the full scope of what we faced. More importantly, we need to understand how we missed it for so long."

He waited as the display lowered from the ceiling. The technology felt incongruous in a room that had hosted war councils since the fifteenth century. The image that appeared on it showed four men at a charity gala, all smiling, all looking harmless. It had been taken recently, perhaps in the last few months.

"The Forgotten Sons," Viper began, taking control of the briefing. "A name that would be pretentious if it weren't so accurate. Four men united by accident of birth and consumed by resentment over what that accident denied them."

She tapped her tablet, and the display shifted to show a complex diagram.

"Before I detail each member, you need to understand the scope of what they built. This wasn't just four bitter men meeting to complain about their brothers. This was a sophisticated operation that took years to construct. Between them, they controlled access to seventeen properties. They had shipping routes through MacKenzie's company that reached every major port in Europe. They had an art market worth forty million pounds annually through Dalgleish's gallery, which provided both funding and money laundering. And through Ambrose, they had something even more valuable—invisibility. The doddering uncle no one took seriously, who could go anywhere, ask anything, and be dismissed as harmless."

Con leaned forward, asking the same question I had. "How did you gather this magnitude of intel between last night and now?"

"I can answer that," said Leila. "So can you, Con."

"It's true that Kestrel helped," said Viper, surprising me with the admission. "As did every agent and operative I could round up from both MI6 and Unit 23." She pointed at Gus. "But Orion deserves the most credit."

He raised his head and looked directly at Leila. "The information was right in front of me. I just had no idea what it all meant. Not until last night."

I'd known him almost all my life and had never seen the expression he held today. It was a combination of regret, sorrow, and guilt for not figuring it out sooner. Not that anyone would have been able to. Later, Con, Ash, and I would make sure he accepted that and let go of the responsibility he'd put on his own shoulders.

Two more photographs appeared. These were older. Typhon pointed at the one on the left, showing Ambrose, Dalgleish, MacKenzie, and MacLeod when they were younger. "This was taken at the Imperial Club," he began. "From what we've been able to piece together, they'd known each other through various social circles." He motioned to the second image. It was of the same four men, but a woman had joined them—Fallon Wallace.

"Chimera played the long game brilliantly," said Viper. "By identifying men with grievances against the system, men who felt cheated by birthright, and she gave them what they'd always wanted—recognition, purpose, and the promise of revenge."

The display changed to show Ambrose's face—not from last night when madness had taken hold, but from a family photo taken at Ash's twenty-first birthday celebration. He stood in the background, smiling, holding a champagne glass, looking exactly like what we'd all believed him to be.

"Let's start with Janus," Viper continued as a more recent photo of him came on the screen. "Ambrose Ashcroft, age sixty-seven. Second son of the late Duke of Ashcroft. His older brother, George, inherited the title as well as all the family's holdings with the exception of a trust fund worth two million pounds that had been set up for Ambrose. It had a modest annuity, enough to be comfortable by most standards, but a fraction of what primogeniture denied him." When she paused, I spoke up.

"You said Wallace brought them together. So she was the driving force? Not Janus?"

"Perhaps in the beginning, but like the rest of us, she may have underestimated Ambrose."

"In the hours before she died, Periscope said, 'Janus thinks he controls Chimera. He's wrong. That may be your only chance at survival.'" Ash turned to Gus. "Your mother said she saw Fallon and Ambrose arguing about something outside Ashcroft."

Gus nodded. "Power struggle, maybe?"

"Based on some of the intel that is still coming in, I'd say that was likely the case," said Typhon. He looked over at Sullivan. "My guess is that the argument was over your abduction. Fallon bringing you into the tunnels beneath Ashcroft had the potential to expose what was really happening down there."

Ash's eyes widened. "What was—or still is—happening down there? Have we found anything?"

Typhon looked at his mobile, then at Ash. "We think it served as a clearing house. Our team is still there, and what they've found looks a lot like what Tag discovered beneath Glenshadow."

My eyes met Con's. "Nothing below Blackmoor yet," he said, answering my unasked question.

Viper cleared her throat. "Back to the briefing," she said, giving Typhon a pointed look, which he scowled at.

The display shifted to show James Dalgleish. Crime scene photos from last night—his body on the castle floor, blood pooling beneath him.

"James Dalgleish," Viper continued. "Age fifty-eight. Second son of the Duke of Moorheath. His older brother, Robert, inherited eleven estates across Scotland, an art collection valued at fifty million pounds, and a seat in the House of Lords that came with considerable political influence. James received a *loan* of five hundred thousand pounds to start his gallery. He built it into an enterprise worth a few million through legitimate sales, but it was never enough. He, like Ambrose, wanted what his brother had been given simply for being born first."

"The gallery was the perfect cover," Gus interjected, looking up from his laptop. "I've been tracking his transactions all night. He'd been moving black market art for years before hooking up with Ambrose. Once they connected, the money coming in grew exponentially. He wasn't just laundering it—he was building a network. Every buyer, every seller, every corrupt customs official became an asset they could use."

The display changed to show shipping manifests and financial records.

"Which brings us to Ian MacKenzie," Viper said. A photo appeared of him at what looked like a corporate event, standing in the shadow of a man who was most likely his brother. "Age fifty-five. Second son of the Duke of Stormbridge. His brother, Donald, inherited the family shipping empire—MacKenzie Lines, worth approximately eight hundred million pounds with routes covering every major port from London to Singapore."

"Ian was given a position as a 'logistics coordinator' in the family company," Typhon said, the contempt clear in his voice. "Middle management in an empire that should have been partially his. His brother made him work for a salary in the company their father built. Every day, Ian had to take orders from men he'd gone to school with, men who knew exactly what he should have been versus what he'd become."

"Humiliating," I murmured, wondering if Cameron and Maggie felt as though I'd cheated them out of our collective birthright. While each had income-generating trusts valued in the millions, perhaps they resented my residency at Glenshadow as well as my control of the majority of our family holdings. I'd always seen it as a responsibility I was forced to take on as the oldest. However, looking at it from their point of view, maybe I had it all wrong.

As if she sensed my discomfort, Leila wrapped her arm through mine and leaned into me. "I love you," she whispered, motioning to where Gus was speaking.

"MacKenzie—Ian, that is—used his position brilliantly, though," he said. "The shipping records I've analyzed show he was moving weapons components for at least three years before AIWS. Small amounts, nothing that would trigger alerts, but it adds up. He created an entire shadow logistics network within his brother's company."

"He's currently in medical custody," Viper added. "Paralyzed from the waist down from his gunshot wound. He's been cooperating fully in exchange for protection—the buyers who lost money on AIWS want blood, and he's an easy target."

The final photo appeared on the display. The kindly estate manager, tears streaming down his weathered face, in what was clearly an interrogation room.

"Fergus MacLeod," Viper said, her tone softening slightly. "This is where the story becomes more complex."

She pulled up a family tree on the display, showing Scottish noble lineages going back centuries.

"The Bramshire dukedom is lesser-known but ancient. The family holdings include three Highland estates and grazing rights to nearly ten thousand acres. Fergus's older brother, Hamish, inherited everything when their father died thirty-five years ago. Hamish's first act was to hire Fergus as estate manager—essentially making him a paid servant on lands that should have been partially his."

"But that wasn't the worst part," Typhon said. "Hamish insisted on paying him a standard salary. A pittance, really, which is why he took on other estates."

"Jesus," Con muttered. "That's cold."

"It gets more complicated," Viper continued. "Fergus married Fiona Campbell twenty-five years ago. She was a schoolteacher from Inverness, who came from a working-class background. Fergus never told her about his noble heritage—he was too ashamed to admit that he was essentially a servant to his own brother. As far as she knew, she'd married a hardworking estate manager who'd pulled himself up by his bootstraps."

"Their daughter Isla never knew, either," Typhon added. "She grew up believing her father was just a dedicated employee who'd saved every penny to send her to university. She's twenty-four now, a marine biologist doing Arctic research in Norway. Her whole life has been built on a lie her father told to protect his pride."

Renegade finally spoke from his place by the window. "My family had no idea that the tunnels beneath Dunravin were being used or that they were even viable."

"No one understands that better than Ash, Con, and I," I told him. "So you're aware, MacLeod did a good job warning us to stay out of them, citing safety concerns."

While he nodded, I sensed he felt the same guilt as the rest of us whose estates were part of Labyrinth's network. It was far worse for Ash, learning the level of Ambrose's involvement.

"I know Isla. We grew up together. She'll be devastated by this," said Renegade.

Viper's expression darkened. "Which raises another concern: her safety and that of her mother. Once we're certain they had no knowledge or involvement with Labyrinth, we'll do whatever we can to make sure there's no fallout for them."

Renegade's mouth gaped. "Once you're *certain*? You can't think—"

"That my uncle was behind one of the most complex and dangerous criminal enterprises in UK history?" Ash stood and paced. "It's no different, Callen, for me or for them. We have a responsibility to carry out the investigation as we would any other."

"Right," Renegade muttered. While I didn't care for his tone and I doubted Viper or Typhon did, either, he deserved the time and space to reconcile the man he grew up believing was a trusted member of Dunravin's staff with the criminal he now knew him to be.

"Moving on," said Viper. "What we've surmised is that MacLeod provided access to several Highland properties for years. Not just Dunravin, but twelve other locations we've now identified. Hidden weapons caches in ancient tunnels, meeting sites in remote locations, safe houses in forgotten corners of Scotland. He knew every hidden passage, every forgotten door, every tunnel that connected these old estates, because he'd spent his whole life exploring them."

"When I was a boy, he'd tell me stories about them," Renegade said quietly. "Jacobite rebels hiding from English soldiers, smugglers moving whiskey, lovers meeting in secret. He made them sound magical."

"If it's any consolation, he appears willing to cooperate," Typhon said. "He's given us everything—names, dates, locations, financial records. He knows he's going to prison, knows his family will be destroyed, but he's trying to minimize the damage."

"What's happening to them?" Leila asked.

"My recommendation is that Fiona and Isla remain in protective custody once we've confirmed their innocence," Viper answered. "Obviously, Mrs. MacLeod is not handling the revelation well. Twenty-five years of marriage built on a fundamental lie, discovering her husband is not just nobility but a terrorist, is a lot to take in."

"Where is Isla?" Renegade asked.

"Returning from Norway under protection. She doesn't know yet. She'll be told when she lands."

He stood abruptly. "She shouldn't hear it from strangers."

"That's not your concern," Viper said.

"I'm making it my concern." His tone brooked no argument. "She doesn't deserve to have her world destroyed by someone reading from a report."

"The buyers who lost money might target her," Typhon warned. "What we're doing ensures her safety."

"I'll take over her detail." Renegade's expression was set. "She's innocent in all of this." He stalked in the direction of the door.

"Hold up, Callen. You're not dismissed," Typhon said, studying him for several seconds. "Let's take this offline and address it after this formal briefing is over."

Renegade's eyes scrunched, and I feared he'd disregard Typhon's direct order. I was relieved when he returned to his previous position by the window.

"Let's resume," Typhon said to Viper, who nodded and brought a map of Scotland up on the display. It showed red markers scattered across the Highlands.

"These are all the locations MacLeod identified," Typhon said. "It will take months to properly secure them all. Some of these tunnels haven't been mapped in centuries. We have no idea what else might be hidden down there."

"The network was more extensive than we imagined," Viper said. "The Forgotten Sons, as they continued to refer to themselves, met regularly at the Imperial Club in Edinburgh. They had codes, procedures, fail-safes we're still uncovering."

"How did McLaren fit into all of this?" Lex asked.

Viper's expression gentled. "We believe she was the person referred to as the Architect, although there is a chance that was an amalgam of more than one person. Years ago, when McLaren initially began her work on AIWS, I do believe her intent was altruistic. After the explosion at the AI facility six months ago, Ambrose knew she meant to destroy Orlov's work that day, and while everyone else was evacuating, he went back for her—not to save her, but to use her. She was injured, disoriented, and he convinced her that he was there to help. By the time she realized the truth, she was imprisoned in a remote location, kept sedated, and controlled through threats against innocent people."

"According to MacLeod, she fought them at every step, at least once she realized he was driven by revenge and greed," Typhon added. "Even while rebuilding AIWS after the explosion and under duress, she added in system weaknesses, back doors, using the very codes that saved us. There came a time when she either knew or sensed Ambrose would eventually kill her, so she made sure someone else could stop him if she couldn't."

"She reached out to Idris," Leila said quietly. "And sent him the codes."

"Your brother died protecting those codes," Viper confirmed. "He never fully understood what they were, but he knew they were important enough to hide. So he embedded them in files only you would treasure—family photos, childhood memories, things that seemed worthless to anyone else but that he knew you'd keep safe."

Even I hadn't known that the encrypted files contained everything Viper had just listed.

The room fell silent, acknowledging the chain of sacrifice—Idris dying to protect something he didn't yet understand, McLaren dying to stop AIWS once and for all, and Leila risking her life in the hope the knowledge she possessed would save our lives and many others.

"The buyers from the gala," I said, breaking the silence. "What's happening to them?"

"Global cooperation unlike anything I've seen," Viper said with grim satisfaction. "Vadim Karpov, the Russian arms dealer, is being extracted to the Hague. Hassan Al-Rashid is in Saudi custody—they're particularly unhappy about his involvement, given the regional implications. Chen Wei is being interrogated by Chinese intelligence, who are very motivated to understand how he nearly caused their infrastructure to collapse."

"They all thought they were buying regional advantage," Typhon explained. "None of them understood that AIWS would have been globally catastrophic. When they realized how close they came to destroying their own countries, cooperation became remarkably easy."

"What about the technology itself?" Gus asked.

Lex stood. "This morning, a courier delivered a packet to me from Evelyn." Her voice caught slightly. "She'd arranged it through her solicitors—a posthumous delivery triggered by her confirmed death. Inside was"—she pulled out a thick envelope from her bag—"complete documentation on AIWS architecture and a systematic protocol for permanent neutralization."

She opened the packet and removed a single document. "She called it a 'cascading corruption sequence.'

It's not just a virus—it's a complete theoretical poisoning of the framework. Any attempt to reconstruct AIWS from surviving fragments will trigger recursive failures. The mathematics themselves become unstable."

"She knew," Lex's voice broke. "She knew she might not survive, so she made sure someone else could destroy her creation for her. The letter says she chose me because I was the only one who understood both the coding architecture and the theoretical physics enough to implement it."

Typhon leaned forward. "Has it been deployed?"

"I initiated it an hour ago," Lex responded. "Every fragment, every backup, every theoretical model—they're all corrupted now. AIWS isn't just dead. It's mathematically impossible to resurrect."

Con squeezed her hand. "She saved millions of lives. That's a legacy worth honoring."

"Brilliant to the end," Lex murmured, wiping away a tear.

"The money trail," Gus said, turning his laptop to show the screen. "I've tracked it all night. The Forgotten Sons had accumulated nearly three hundred million pounds through various channels—arms sales, money laundering through Dalgleish's gallery, extortion, blackmail. It's been seized and frozen. International courts will determine distribution, but most will go to victims' funds."

"Victims?" Ash asked. "I thought Nightingale stopped it last night."

"The explosion at the AI facility killed twelve people," Typhon told him. "The weapons the Forgotten Sons trafficked before AIWS killed hundreds in various conflicts. There are always victims, even when we prevent the worst."

"The public story," Con said. "How are we containing this?"

"Official version is a gas leak at Brodick Castle during the Highland Heritage Gala," Viper answered. "Four dead, several injured. Dalgleish's family is being told a version closer to the truth—that he was involved in terrorism and was stopped by security forces. MacKenzie survived and will eventually stand trial. MacLeod will also face prosecution, but his cooperation is being considered. This operation is being classified beyond top secret," she added. "The public can never know how close we came to global catastrophe. It would cause panic, undermine faith in institutions, and potentially trigger the very chaos we prevented."

"But the people who matter know," Typhon said, looking at each of us. "The Prime Minister, the Crown, allied intelligence agencies—they know what you all did. You won't get public recognition, but you have the gratitude of everyone who understands what almost happened."

"We don't do it for recognition," said Con.

"No," Typhon agreed. "But you've earned it, nonetheless. Take a week. All of you. Rest, recover, process what's happened. The world will still need saving when you return, but for now, let others handle it."

After Typhon and Viper left the room to meet with Renegade, the formal atmosphere dissolved. Con slumped in his chair, pulling Lex against him. Gus closed his laptop for the first time in hours. Ash and Sullivan were quiet. Too quiet.

"Fuck," Con said eloquently.

"Yeah," Gus agreed. "That about covers it."

Leila stood, wincing. "I need to see him."

"Who?" I asked, though I suspected I knew.

"MacLeod. I need to understand why someone who was kind to us could do this."

"That's not a good idea—"

"I need to, Tag." Her eyes were fierce despite the exhaustion. "He warned us, fed us, tried to protect us even while betraying us. I need to understand how someone can be both things at once."

I recognized the look—she wouldn't be dissuaded.

"I'll arrange it," I said. "But I'm coming with you."

"I wouldn't want you anywhere else."

The rest of the day passed in a blur of arrangements and quiet conversations, including one very frank one with my brother and sister that we agreed to continue over the course of the next few days with an intended goal of dividing the estate, along with its responsibilities, among the three of us.

Renegade returned to London with Viper and Typhon, presumably to meet Isla's flight, although nothing official was said.

That evening, after everyone other than Cameron and Maggie left, we gathered not in the formal dining room but in the kitchen, where Mrs. Murrey held court. She'd made all our favorite foods from childhood but included a special surprise just for Leila—Sticky Toffee Pudding.

"How did you know my mother's secret ingredient?" she asked after savoring the first spoonful.

"A not-so-wee sparrow whispered in my ear," our housekeeper teased.

My eyes met Leila's. "Typhon," we said at the same time.

The storm had passed, but its effects would ripple for months, maybe years. Trials to attend, testimonies to give, the slow work of justice grinding forward. But tonight, we were alive, we were together, and the world still turned.

Tomorrow would bring its own challenges. Tonight was enough.

19

Nightingale

Two weeks had passed since Brodick Castle, and the bruises on my throat had faded from purple to yellow-green. The ones on my ribs still ached when I breathed too deeply, but they were healing. Everything was healing, slowly.

Tag had been diligent about arranging for us to visit MacLeod, but he was still being held in a secret location, spilling more details about Project Labyrinth. His wife and daughter were out of protective custody now that the buyers had been arrested, but Renegade said they weren't ready for visitors. Maybe I wasn't ready either.

I pushed the thought away. Today wasn't about MacLeod or his betrayals. Today was about Idris.

As the private jet descended through clouds toward Damascus, my heart clenched. The city spread out below us—ancient stone and modern glass creating a tapestry that still took my breath away. I pressed my face to the window, watching familiar landmarks appear. The Umayyad Mosque's minaret. Mount Qasioun looming over everything. The old city walls that had stood for centuries.

"There. That's where we lived."

Tag leaned over to look. "Where? I don't see any buildings."

"No, they're gone. Destroyed in the conflict. But that park—" I pointed at a small green space. "Idris taught me to ride a bicycle there."

The plane touched down smoothly, and soon, we were in an armored SUV, winding through Damascus' streets. The city had changed since my last visit. More reconstruction, fewer checkpoints. Still scarred but healing, like me.

"The tea shop," I blurted, spotting a familiar storefront. "Can we stop?"

The driver looked to Tag, who nodded. Inside, the elderly owner looked up from his newspaper, his face lighting with recognition.

"Leila?"

"Hello, Uncle Mahmoud." He wasn't really my uncle, but in Damascus, all family friends of a certain age were aunts and uncles.

He came around the counter and embraced me. "I wondered if I'd ever see you again, *habibti*."

"I need Ahmad's Blend," I said, naming the tea Idris had loved. "Loose."

Understanding crossed his face. He prepared a small bag containing the blend I'd requested—sage, mint, and black tea that Idris would buy weekly. The smell brought back mornings in our kitchen.

"No charge," Uncle Mahmoud said when I reached for my wallet.

I kissed his cheeks in thanks and returned to the SUV, clutching the small bag like a talisman.

The cemetery where my brother was buried sat on a hill outside the city, surrounded by olive trees. The security detail who'd accompanied us from the airfield spread out, giving us space while maintaining a perimeter. Tag carried the flowers I'd chosen—white roses for purity, purple irises for valor, and baby's breath for everlasting love. I carried the tea and a small bottle of Turkish coffee I'd bought at the airport.

Idris' grave stood in the eastern corner, facing Mecca. It was simple and white. No name was shown, but I still knew it. I'd always know it.

Beloved Son and Brother

In every blade of grass is the story of the universe.

The quote was Rumi, of course. I traced the letters with trembling fingers.

"Hello, brother," I whispered. "The codes you left me—you saved the world." My voice broke. "McLaren died activating them, but she knew I had them because of you. She said 'Damascus codes' with her last breath, and I understood because you hid them in memories of Damascus. Of us."

I opened the bag of tea, sprinkling some over the grave—an old tradition our father had taught us. The coffee came next, poured in a small circle around the headstone.

"Your favorite," I said. "Too much sugar, just how you liked it. The man responsible for your death is dead. The network behind him is destroyed. Justice isn't the same as having you back, but it's something."

Tag knelt beside me, placing the flowers against the stone. "Rest well, brother," he said in Arabic—a phrase I'd taught him.

"Thank you," I whispered to the stone. "For teaching me to be brave. For loving me. For leading me to the man you trusted. Who loves me as much as I love him."

A wind swept through the olive trees, and for just a moment, I could almost hear an oud playing somewhere in the distance. It was probably my imagination, but it made me smile.

We stayed for a few more minutes in respectful silence, then walked back through the cemetery hand in hand. But instead of returning directly to the city, Tag asked the driver to take the mountain road.

"Where are we going?"

"You'll see."

The road wound up Mount Qasioun, and I realized where he was taking me—it was the same overlook where Idris had brought me when I was sixteen, where all of Damascus spread out like a jewel box. We stopped at a pull-off, and Tag dismissed the security detail to a respectful distance.

The city lay before us, golden in the late-afternoon light. The same view Idris had shown me all those years ago. "Remember where you come from," he'd said. "But don't let it limit where you go."

"You knew about this place?" I asked Tag.

"Idris mentioned it once. He said it was special to the two of you."

We sat on the ancient stone wall, legs dangling over the edge like children. The silence between us was comfortable, filled with the distant sounds of the city below—car horns, the call to prayer, life continuing despite everything.

"Leila?" The way he said my name made me turn to face him, and when I did, I watched as he pulled a small velvet box from his pocket.

"Tag?"

He opened the lid, revealing an antique ring—an emerald surrounded by diamonds in a Celtic design that looked ancient and precious.

"This was my grandmother's," he said. "Hers and my grandfather's was the only happy marriage in three generations of MacTaggerts. Before she died, she told me to give it to the woman who made me want to be better than I was."

Tears blurred my vision as he continued.

"I know we're complicated. Our work is dangerous, our lives are unconventional. But when I thought I'd lost you at Brodick, nothing else mattered. Not the mission, not protocols, not the world ending. Just you." He took a breath. "Marry me, Leila. Not because Idris asked me to protect you, but because I love you. Because you make me brave enough to believe we can forge our own path, make our own way, not repeating the mistakes of the past."

I looked at the ring, at Tag's face, at the city spread below—my past and my future colliding in this moment.

"My parents failed because they gave up," Tag said. "I promise you I will never give up on us."

"Yes," I said.

"Yes?"

"Yes." Stronger now. "Yes, to all of it—the love and the complicated, messy, beautiful life we'll build."

His hands shook as he slipped the ring onto my finger. The emerald caught the setting sun, throwing green sparks that reminded me of Tag's eyes. Then he was kissing me, and I was laughing and crying at the same time.

When we finally broke apart, I looked back toward the cemetery, hidden now behind the hills.

"He would have been happy about this," I said. "Idris. He always said I needed someone as stubborn as me."

"He also said you needed someone who could cook. I'm thinking I might need lessons."

I laughed. "That's what Mrs. Murray is for."

On the return trip to the airport, I kept looking at the ring, then at the man who, one day soon, would be my husband.

"Glenshadow or London?" Tag asked as the SUV pulled onto the tarmac.

"What?"

"To live."

I smiled. "Glenshadow for home. London for work."

"Agreed."

As we boarded the plane that would take us to Edinburgh, I looked back at Damascus one more time. This city of memory and loss, of beginnings and endings.

"Are you sure you don't want to stay longer?" Tag asked.

"I've done all I came to do." I nudged him. "And more," I added with a wink as I held up my left hand.

The return trip was quiet. We sat together in comfortable silence, my hand in his, the ring catching the cabin lights.

"June," I blurted.

"June?"

"For the wedding. June at Glenshadow. It should be small."

"Agreed."

As the plane began its descent, I watched Scotland appear through the clouds—green and gray and nothing like Damascus, but home now in a way I hadn't expected.

"I love you," I said.

"I love you too," Tag replied.

The words were simple, but they carried so much weight. We'd almost lost everything at Brodick. We'd saved the world but nearly destroyed ourselves in the process. And somehow, we'd found this—this promise of a future neither of us had thought possible.

The plane touched down at Edinburgh's private airfield, where a helicopter waited on the tarmac, ready to take us to Glenshadow. As we walked to it, Tag squeezed my hand.

"Ready for Mrs. Murray's reaction?"

"She'll cry."

"Definitely."

"And then immediately start planning menus."

"Without question."

We climbed into the chopper, and as it lifted off, I watched the city fall away below us. Somewhere down there, ordinary people were living ordinary lives, never knowing how close they'd come to losing everything.

The ring felt heavy on my finger—not uncomfortable, just significant. A choice made. A future claimed.

The Highlands appeared through the mist, and with them, Glenshadow. Home.

Epilogue

Tag

Six months later

The morning of my wedding day dawned clear and cold, mist rising from the loch like something out of legend. I stood at my bedroom window in Glenshadow, watching the sunrise while adjusting my suit and tie for the dozenth time.

"You're going to wear out the fabric," said Con.

I turned to find my best man standing in the doorway, looking amused. Behind him, Ash and Gus struggled with their bow ties.

"Here." Con stepped forward to help them. "Honestly, you can disarm a bomb but can't manage formal wear?"

"Bombs are simpler," Gus muttered.

"I'm not on the bloody bomb squad," Ash muttered.

They'd been trying to keep the mood light all morning, for my sake and Ash's. This was his first formal event since Ambrose's death. He'd lost weight, and shadows lingered under his eyes, but he'd insisted on being here.

"Sullivan?" I asked him.

"On her way."

A knock at the door interrupted us, and Douglas entered with a silver tray.

"Whiskey, gentlemen. The twenty-five-year Macallan."

"Bit early, isn't it?" Gus asked.

"It's tradition," I said, accepting a glass. "My grandfather started it. A toast with the groomsmen before facing matrimony."

We raised our glasses.

"To Tag," Con said. "Who finally found someone as stubborn as him."

"To Leila," Ash added. "Who saved the world and still agreed to marry you."

"To the future," Gus contributed. "Whatever it brings."

"To family," I said, looking at each of them. "Blood or chosen."

We drank, the whiskey burning warm down my throat.

"Speaking of family," Con said, setting down his glass. "Did you know Leila invited the MacLeods?"

"What?" Ash gasped.

"Fiona and the daughter. They're here."

"Christ," Gus muttered.

"That's my wife-to-be," I said. "She believes in redemption. Or at least in not punishing the innocent."

"The daughter just got back from Norway, didn't she?" Con asked. "Renegade mentioned something about it being complicated. Research station in the Arctic or something."

"From what we've been able to ascertain, she had nothing to do with her father's crimes," I confirmed.

"Still," Ash said quietly. "Can't be easy for them, being here."

"Or easy for everyone else, having them here," Con added.

"We've all done things," I reminded them. "Or had family who did things. Glass houses and all that."

Gus checked his watch. "Right, then. Philosophy later. Time to get you married."

The chapel at Glenshadow had stood for four hundred years, witness to countless MacTaggert ceremonies—christenings, weddings, funerals. Today, it had been transformed with white roses and purple heather, Leila's choices. Simple but elegant, like her.

The guests were already assembled as my friends and I took our positions at the altar. A small gathering by any standard—Unit 23-ers, select MI6 personnel, a few trusted friends. It was perfect.

Typhon sat in the second row with his wife, Eliza. Beside her, Viper dabbed at her eyes with a hand-kerchief, though she'd deny it later. Mrs. Murray sat across the aisle, already weeping openly but silently. Douglas stood at the back like a sentry.

I spotted Fiona MacLeod in the last row, wearing simple black, her face carefully composed. Beside her sat a young woman with auburn hair pulled back severely—Isla. She stared straight ahead, her posture rigid, as if she was enduring rather than attending. Renegade sat beside them.

The music changed, and everyone stood.

First came Lex as maid of honor, radiant in deep purple.

Then, when Leila appeared, everything else faded.

She wore a simple white dress that managed to be both elegant and practical, and her dark hair was swept up. Her eyes found mine, and the smile that spread across her face made my heart stop. This was happening. We were doing this.

She walked alone, because as she'd said, she was giving herself to me.

When she reached me, I took her hands, feeling a tremor in them that matched my own.

"You clean up nicely, MacTaggert," she murmured.

"You're beautiful," I replied, meaning it with every fiber of my being.

The ceremony itself was simple. Traditional vows with a few modifications—we'd removed "obey" and added "support in all missions, classified or otherwise," which got a laugh from those who understood.

"Do you, Niall MacTaggert, take Leila Nassar to be your wife?" the officiant asked.

"I do." No hesitation.

"Do you, Leila Nassar, take Niall MacTaggert to be your husband?"

"I do." Clear and certain.

"The rings?"

Con produced the simple platinum bands we'd chosen together. No inscriptions that could be used for identification if we were captured. Practical even in romance.

As I slipped the ring onto her finger, next to the emerald engagement ring, I said the words we'd written together. "From the storms of Dunravin to the towers of Brodick, through every mission and every morning, you are my partner, my equal, my love. I promise to trust you, to support you, and to never stop choosing us."

Her eyes glistened as she put the other ring on my finger. "You taught me that love isn't weakness but strength. That partnership means standing together, especially when we disagree. You are my anchor, my challenger, my home. I promise to fight for us, to believe in us, and to love you through whatever comes."

"By the power vested in me, I pronounce you husband and wife. You may kiss—"

I didn't let him finish. I pulled Leila against me, kissing her thoroughly while our friends cheered and laughed. She kissed me back just as fiercely, not caring about propriety or tradition.

When we finally broke apart, she whispered, "Hello, husband."

"Hello, wife."

Rose petals fell around us as we walked back down the aisle—the guests throwing them with enthusiasm.

Glenshadow's great hall had been transformed with lights and flowers into the most magical of places for our celebration. The speeches ranged from touching—Con talking about partnership forged in fire—to embarrassing. I barely paid attention, too focused on my bride, until Typhon stood, commanding attention without effort.

"I've overseen hundreds of partnerships in my career," he began. "Most are professional. Some become friendships. Very few become what these two have—a bond that saved millions of lives because they trusted each other when it mattered most. As Con said, the best partnerships are forged in fire, but I'll add that they are sustained in peace. May you have both in equal measure."

As the evening progressed, Viper pulled Leila and me aside. "I hate to interrupt, but there's something you should know."

"If you're about to assign us a mission on our wedding day—" Leila started.

"No, nothing like that. But there's been chatter. Someone's been asking questions about the Forgotten Sons, about what really happened at Brodick."

"Press?"

"Unknown. Just be aware. Even on your honeymoon. Maldives, right? Beautiful beaches, terrible sight lines, multiple aquatic approach vectors."

"We'll be careful," I promised.

"I know you will." She squeezed Leila's hand. "Enjoy your happiness. You've earned it."

The party continued late into the night. At one point, I found Ash outside.

"Thank you for being here," I said.

"I wouldn't have missed it. You know that."

"Still."

"Brose made his choice. My only regret is not paying more attention. Not that I believe it would've done any good." I watched him return to Sullivan's side. For too many years, my friend had been a loner. More so than Con, Gus, and me. Knowing he had his wife's support as he navigated his uncle's betrayal lessened my worry about him.

"What are you thinking?" I asked my wife, wrapping my arms around her from behind.

"That Idris would have loved today. The ceremony, the people, you—us."

"I think he was here, in the love you carry for him."

She turned in my arms. "That's deeply romantic coming from you."

"You bring out the best in me."

She kissed me then, slow and deep. "Take me to bed, husband."

"With pleasure, wife."

Later, tangled in sheets and each other, I thought about the cycle of loss and love that had brought us here. The future spinning out before us, unknown but no longer feared.

"Tag?" Leila's voice was drowsy.

"Yes, my love?"

"Thank you."

"For what?"

"For not giving up. For choosing us."

"Always."

Outside, wind rattled the ancient windows of Glenshadow. Somewhere in the sky on their way back to London, Viper and Typhon were tracking whatever new threat had emerged. The world kept spinning, but here, now, in this moment, we were just Tag and Leila. Husband and wife. Partners in every sense.

It was enough. It was everything.

"I love you," I said into the darkness.

"I love you," she replied. "Forever."

It was a dangerous word in our line of work, just like promises were. But we'd chosen to face whatever came our way together. "Yes, forever," I said, leaning down to kiss her forehead.

When sleep came, I dreamed of white-sand beaches, long days spent making love under the sun, and the swell of Leila's stomach when the child—children—we'd create together arrived to join us.

Forever, indeed.

Keep reading for a sneak peek at
the first book in Merrigan Calder's
Thorned Thistle Series
which features characters from the
Protectors Undercover Team One Series,
***Commanded: A Thorned
Thistle Dark Romance***

***At a remote Highland estate,
a commanding dominant offers two
broken souls sanctuary—and a chance to surrender to the darkest desires
they've denied themselves.***

GREYMARCH

I see what they hide the moment they arrive—Prima's desperate need to surrender beneath her masks, Vanguard's craving to submit hidden under all that dominance. I want to strip away every false layer and claim them both. What I don't anticipate is how commanding them will leave me just as exposed.

VANGUARD

I hadn't questioned who I was until I discovered the Thorned Thistle, near the estate where we've taken refuge. My attraction to Greymarch confuses me, and my need to protect Prima while surrendering to him terrifies me. Between them, I'm forced to accept a truth I've been running from: I crave the surrender as much as the control.

PRIMA

I've spent my life performing, becoming whoever others need me to be. But Greymarch sees through every mask, and Vanguard protects me like I'm worth saving. Between commanding dominance and fierce devotion, I can finally stop thinking and just feel. For the first time, I can surrender to what I've always craved.

Prima

"Don't move." The voice of the man who'd commanded I call him Greymarch when we were in this place cut through the dim light of the Thorned Thistle's private viewing room, and I froze with my hand halfway to the door handle.

"You weren't going to leave without saying goodbye, were you, Ophelia?"

I hated how he said my real name. Like he knew all my secrets. Like he owned them.

"I need to go," I whispered, but my traitorous body wouldn't turn the handle.

"No."

"But—"

"You're done running."

I heard him move closer, felt his heat behind me. He didn't touch me—he never touched without permission—but I could feel him everywhere.

"He's looking for you," the man who could read my every thought said, making my pulse jump. "Downstairs. Prowling the main floor like a hunter."

"I know." My voice came out breathy, desperate.

"You left him hard and aching in the library after that little performance of yours."

My face burned. "It wasn't a performance."

"No?" His breath stirred my hair. "Then, what would you call grinding against him while you watched me demonstrate rope work with another submissive? What would you call the way you moaned when I met your eyes across the room?"

"Stop."

"That isn't your safe word."

God help me, it wasn't. We'd established it three nights ago, when I agreed to this insanity. When I'd agreed to explore what it meant to want two men at once. What it meant to want to kneel for them.

"Turn around."

I did because I always did what he commanded. Long before he brought me here. It was how he knew. And that was why I needed to leave.

He stood too close, dressed in black leather pants and nothing else, his chest still gleaming with sweat—the laird who'd become the Highlands' most infamous dominant. The man who saw through every mask I wore.

"You're scared," he stated as simply as he'd told me no.

"Yes."

"Of me?"

"Of what you make me want."

His smile was dark, too knowing. "And what about what he makes you want?"

As if summoned, the door opened behind me and someone walked in. I didn't have to turn to know who it was. I could smell his cologne and feel the way the air changed when he entered a room.

"Going somewhere, Prima?" he asked.

My code name on his lips was a reminder of what we were outside these walls. Operatives. Pro-fessionals. Not… whatever this was becoming.

"I—"

"She was running." Greymarch's distant gaze looked at nothing, yet saw everything. "Again." He stepped forward, less than an inch from me. My nip-ples hardened instantly.

The other man moved behind me, trapping me between their bodies. Still not touching, but so close I could barely breathe.

"We talked about this." His voice was rough. "No running. No hiding. Not here."

"This is getting too complicated."

"Because you want us both?" Greymarch asked. "Or because we both want you?"

My breath caught. In three nights of watching, of learning, of careful negotiations, we'd danced around the truth. That this wasn't just about me exploring submission. It was about the three of us starting something that shouldn't work but did.

"Tell us to stop," the man behind me said. "Use your safe word, and this ends. We go back to being colleagues who share a secret."

I opened my mouth, but the word wouldn't come.

Greymarch's leather-clad thigh brushed my hip when he closed the space between us. "Or tell us the truth."

"What truth?"

"That you've been wet since you watched me bind her. That you imagined it was you in those ropes, suspended and helpless while he watched." Greymarch's voice dropped lower. "That you've been pressing your thighs together, trying to find relief, but what you really need is permis-sion."

My eyes drifted closed. "Please." I said the word, unsure what I was asking for.

"Please what?" The voice behind me had gone commanding. "Please let you go? Or please make you stay?"

"I don't know."

"Liar." Greymarch's finger traced my cheek. "You know exactly what you want. You're just too afraid to ask for it."

"What if someone finds out? What if—"

"What if you stop living in fear?" he interrupted. "What if you actually let yourself have what you want for once in your perfectly controlled life?"

Hands gripped me from behind. Rough. Less practiced. But no less possessive.

"We've been dancing around this for days," the voice said against my ear. "Watching scenes, talking about limits, pretending this is just curiosity. But we all know what happens next."

"What?" My voice was barely a whisper.

Greymarch smiled, dark and full of promise. "You choose. Submit to what you want, or walk out that door and we never speak of this again."

I stood there, caught between them, between worlds, between who I believed myself to be and who I was in this place where masks didn't matter.

"If I stay..."

"You have twenty-four hours to make your decision. If you stay, then tomorrow night, you're ours. No more watching. No more talking. Just feeling."

"Yours?"

"Isn't that what you want?" The hands on my waist tightened. "Both of us learning exactly what makes you fall apart? What makes you beg? What makes you scream?"

I shuddered. "Yes." The word escaped before I could stop it.

"Yes, what?" Greymarch's voice was pure command.

"Yes, Sir."

"And?" He nodded toward the man behind me.

I turned my head, meeting those dangerous eyes that had haunted my dreams for months. "Yes, Sir."

His pupils went black. "Fuck."

"Tomorrow," Greymarch said firmly. "Here. We'll be waiting."

"What should I—"

"Wear something you don't mind losing." His smile turned wicked as he stepped away at the same time the man at my back walked to the opposite side of the room. "We have three days of frustrated want to work through. Your clothes won't survive it."

The sound that came from deep inside me didn't feel human.

"Go," Greymarch commanded. "Before we decide we can't let you."

I fumbled for the door handle, desperate to escape before I begged them not to let me go. Before I dropped to my knees and admitted how badly I needed this.

"Ophelia?"

I paused at Greymarch's voice.

"Touch yourself tonight if you need to. But don't come. Not until we give you permission."

The door clicked shut on my desperate whimper.

Tomorrow night, everything would change.

Tomorrow night, I would finally stop running.

Tomorrow night, I would be theirs.

About the Author

USA Today best-selling author Heather Slade writes shamelessly sexy, edge-of-your seat romantic suspense.

She gave herself the gift of writing a book for her own birthday one year. Seventy-plus books later (and counting), she's having the time of her life.

The women Slade writes are self-confident, strong, with wills of their own, and hearts as big as the Colorado sky. The men are sublimely sexy, seductive alphas who rise to the challenge of capturing the sweet soul of a woman whose heart they'll hold in the palm of their hand forever. Add in a couple of neck-snapping twists and turns, a page-turning mystery, and a swoon-worthy HEA, and you'll be holding one of her books in your hands.

She loves to hear from her readers. You can contact her at heather@heatherslade.com

To keep up with her latest news and releases, please visit her website at www.heatherslade.com to sign up for her newsletter.

MORE FROM AUTHOR HEATHER SLADE

BUTLER RANCH
Kade's Worth
Brodie's Promise
Maddox's Truce
Naughton's Secret
Mercer's Vow
Kade's Return
Butler Ranch Christmas

WICKED WINEMAKERS
FIRST LABEL
Brix's Bid
Ridge's Release
Press' Passion
Zin's Sins
Tryst's Temptation

WICKED WINEMAKERS
SECOND LABEL
Beau's Beloved
Cru's Crush
Bit's Bliss
Snapper's Seduction
Kick's Kiss

ROARING FORK RANCH
Roaring Fork Wrangler
Roaring Fork Roughstock
Roaring Fork Rockstar
Roaring Fork Rooker
Roaring Fork Bridger

PROTECTORS
UNDERCOVER TEAM ONE
Undercover Agent
Undercover Emissary
Undercover Savior
Undercover Infidel
Undercover Shadow

THE ROYAL AGENTS
OF MI6
Make Me Shiver
Drive Me Wilder
Feel My Pinch
Chase My Shadow
Find My Angel

K19 SECURITY
SOLUTIONS TEAM ONE
Razor's Edge
Gunner's Redemption
Mistletoe's Magic
Mantis' Desire
Dutch's Salvation

K19 SECURITY
SOLUTIONS TEAM TWO
Striker's Choice
Monk's Fire
Halo's Oath
Tackle's Honor
Onyx's Awakening

K19 SHADOW OPERATIONS
TEAM ONE
Code Name: Ranger
Code Name: Diesel
Code Name: Wasp
Code Name: Cowboy
Code Name: Mayhem

K19 ALLIED INTELLIGENCE
TEAM ONE
Code Name: Ares
Code Name: Cayman
Code Name: Poseidon
Code Name: Zeppelin
Code Name: Magnet

K19 ALLIED INTELLIGENCE
TEAM TWO
Code Name: Puck
Code Name: Michelangelo
Code Name: Typhon
Code Name: Hornet
Code Name: Reaper

MINERVA PROTOCOL
Phoenix Ascent
Shield Stratagem
Ghost Matrix
Compass Initiative
Decree Directive

K19 SENTINEL CYBER
TEAM ONE
Code Name: Admiral
Code Name: Dante
Code Name: Grit
Code Name: Tank
Code Name: Atticus

K19 SENTINEL CYBER
TEAM TWO
Code Name: Kodiak
Code Name: Paragon
Code Name: Vex
Code Name: Jagger
Code Name: Shredder

THE INVINCIBLES
TEAM ONE
Code Name: Deck
Code Name: Edge
Code Name: Grinder
Code Name: Rile
Code Name: Smoke

THE INVINCIBLES
TEAM TWO
Code Name: Buck
Code Name: Irish
Code Name: Saint
Code Name: Hammer
Code Name: Rip

THE UNSTOPPABLES
TEAM ONE
Code Name: Fury
Code Name: Married

COWBOYS OF
CRESTED BUTTE
A Cowboy Falls
A Cowboy's Dance
A Cowboy's Kiss
A Cowboy Stays
A Cowboy Wins